John C. Clyde

History of the First Presbyterian Church of Bloomsbury, New Jersey

with a preliminary sketch of the neighborhood from its earliest settlement

John C. Clyde

History of the First Presbyterian Church of Bloomsbury, New Jersey
with a preliminary sketch of the neighborhood from its earliest settlement

ISBN/EAN: 9783337367749

Printed in Europe, USA, Canada, Australia, Japan

Cover: Foto ©Andreas Hilbeck / pixelio.de

More available books at **www.hansebooks.com**

HISTORY

OF THE

FIRST PRESBYTERIAN CHURCH

OF

BLOOMSBURY, NEW JERSEY,

WITH

A PRELIMINARY SKETCH OF THE NEIGHBORHOOD FROM ITS EARLIEST SETTLEMENT.

BY

REV. JOHN C. CLYDE, A. M.,

Author of History of the Allen Township or Irish Settlement Presbyterian Church, Penn.; Genealogies, Necrology and Reminiscences of the Irish Settlement; Life, Labors and Death of Rev. John Rosbrugh, Clerical Martyr of the Revolution; Life of Prof. James H. Coffin, LL.D., of Lafayette College.

BLOOMSBURY:
PUBLISHED BY SUBSCRIPTION.
1884.

PREFACE.

The following pages were prepared in pursuance of the recommendation of the General Assembly of 1881, wherein, among other things, aid was solicited for the Presbyterian Historical Society in its work of collecting "Histories and discourses concerning churches, &c." The manuscript, after being prepared, was read to the congregation, in installments, during the months of July and August, 1883. Subsequently, through the efforts chiefly of Hon. H. R. Kennedy, an elder in the church, who secured the list of subscribers whose names are appended to the work, the way was opened for its appearance in the present printed form.

In the preparation of the history we have followed the records of the trustees, session and higher church courts, where material was to be found suitable to our purpose. We have also laid under tribute the histories of Hunterdon and Warren counties, and such other secular records as were calculated to aid us in the task undertaken. Outside of these, we are, more than to any other, indebted to Mr. Kennedy for valuable information, especially so with reference to the preliminary chapter, wherein is sketched the characteristics of the neighborhood from its earliest settlement down to the organization of the Bloomsbury church. Acknowledging these aids, and also the kindness of the subscribers in opening the way for the publication of the history, we send it forth conscious of its many imperfections, but with the hope that it may be of some interest to the church and to the community at large.

J. C. C.

BLOOMSBURY, N. J., *December*, 1883.

CONTENTS.

—— 0 ——

HISTORY.

—— o ——

CHAPTER I.
PRELIMINARY HISTORY.

*General principles affecting communities.   Natural surroundings.   First set-
tlers.   The Robert Johnston tract of land south of the Musconetcong.   The John
Cook tract north of the Musconetcong, subsequently held by the Heanries, Kenne-
dys and others.   Village of Bloomsbury.   Early education of community.   Ec-
clesiastical antecedents.   Rise and progress of Methodism.*

The student of ethnology learns at a very early stage of his investi-
gations that circumstances largely determine the different characteristics which we see among the various parts of the human family.   A
river, by its even flow, and by its supply of a prime necessary of life,
forms an avenue along which man finds it easy to travel, either by
floating upon its bosom or by journeying upon its banks.   We see the
migration of mankind therefore governed largely by the courses of the
streams by which the earth is watered.   A mountain, by its precipitous
sides and lack of those things which minister most conveniently to
man's daily wants, becomes a barrier by which he is confined to certain
limits, or his course of migration is deflected.   The opening of public
roads through the country and the construction of railroads, thus facili-
tating the intercourse between mankind, constitute a powerful factor
in determining the mobility of communities and the formation of cen-

tees of population and trade. The fertile valley, which is planted as a garden amid charming surrounding scenery, and which yields a satisfying return to the husbandman for his toil, thus making him prosperous and happy, is a powerful incentive in developing the intellectual and physical nature of man. On the other hand the barren and broken regions—the waste places of the earth—which have nothing to attract the eye or cheer the heart, have a tendency to dull the intellectual perceptions, and stunt the growth of the physical man. Again, the influences brought to bear upon mankind through education, intellectual and moral, in conjunction with physical surroundings, are large factors in determining the condition of a community at any given period of its history. If the people have had the advantages of good secular education and wholesome moral training, they will be found, as a rule, possessing a proportionate amount of wealth, intellectual power and disposition to accomplish commendable things in political, social, and religious life. If, on the other hand, their means of secular education have been limited, and their moral training neglected, they will be found to be, as a rule, incapable of preserving from waste what nature by the operation of her laws may have provided for them, and possessed of little inclination to put forth efforts for advancement politically, socially or religiously.

In arriving at a true historical estimate of a church, therefore, at any given period of its existence, such things as these must be taken into consideration. We find then, with reference to the First Presbyterian Church of Bloomsbury, that nature has done much to help her on to success. When we survey the physical characteristics of the section of country occupied by the congregation we see what advantages it has had in location, to make it compact and prosperous. Through the midst of it flows the beautiful, rapid, clear and cold waters of the Musconetcong creek. Its waters have ever ministered to the comfort, happiness, and prosperity of the people. Upon its banks they have ever wended their way either in the pursuits of every day life, or for the purpose of worshiping God. On the south is seen the picturesque range of the Musconetcong mountains, clad as they are in richest green in summer or purest white in winter, dotted with the fields, orchards, and farm houses of the industrious and frugal inhabitants, and holding in its bosom rich deposits of iron, which ministers so largely to man's prosperity, convenience and happiness. To the north may be seen the lower and more broken Pohatcong range which forms the natural boundary between the Musconetcong and Pohatcong valleys. Down the valley, at a distance of about a mile from the church, the the hills close in upon each other, thus forming in this part of the valley what might be called a *cul de sac* or pocket, thus forming a natural boundary to the congregation on the southwest and west. So completely closed in is the congregation in this direction that the Musconetcong creek struggles through a deep ravine, with scarcely room for a foot path upon its banks, as it impetuously rushes over its rocky bed to mingle its waters with those of the Delaware. To the northeast, or up the stream, stretches the unbroken surface of the valley, having merged into it, ten or twelve miles distant, the Pohatcong valley, and thus holding its course to the northeast till it is lost in the hill country of Sussex county.

The part of the valley occupied by the Bloomsbury congregation is a "rich alluvial with mixture of red shale which returns large crops to the husbandman." "It is a pretty well established fact that the first white settlers of the township [of Bethlehem, Hunterdon county, in which the church is located] were Hollanders, and came here in the early part of the last century. Among the descendants of the pioneer settlers who still retain a portion at least of the original purchases, are the Hoffmans, Alpaughs, Crevelings, Hoppocks, Duckworths, Willevers, Vliets, Boss, Housels, Opdykes and others whose ancestors were pioneers along the river." "That part of the township immediately around Bloomsbury has come down through the possession of Robert Johnston, who owned a large tract including not only what is now the village of Bloomsbury, but the farms of Moses Robins and John Stute on the west, and the Taylor property on the east of the village and running to the top of the mountain. The Taylor tract was probably the eastern part of this original tract of Robert Johnston. A little further east was a tract owned for a short time by a man named Hamilton; then came tracts, a part of which are still in possession of the descendants of the original owners, as previously stated." *His. Hun. Co.* 1881, *pp.* 457, 458.

The section thus described substantially covers the ground occupied by that portion of the congregation lying south of the Musconetcong creek, i. e. in Hunterdon county.

When we pass to the portion lying north of the creek and between it and the Pohatcong range, which divides the Musconetcong from the Pohatcong valley, we find that John Cook of Frankford, Pennsylvania, had surveyed to him by Samuel Green, on a writ from the Council of Proprietors of the Western Division of the Province of New Jersey, one thousand one hundred and eleven acres of land in Greenwich township, county of Hunterdon, (as it then was) fronting on the "Musconekonk River" near Silver Hill, and the rear on "Pohatkong Brook." The survey of this tract of land was recorded in the Surveyor General's Office at Burlington, bearing date June 2. 1715.

Hannah Cook, granddaughter of John Cook, to whom the above tract was surveyed, together with her husband William Heanrie, living in the township of Greenwich, conveyed, by deed bearing date Dec. 6. 1742, to Adam Hall and Elisabeth his wife, five hundred acres of the lower or western portion of this tract of land; and Adam Hall and wife, by deed bearing date Deb. 16. 1742, conveyed three hundred and thirty-three and one third acres of the lower portion of the five hundred acres, and fronting on the "Musconekong River," to Christopher Falconberger; and Mr. Falconberger acquired by deed bearing date Oct. 10. 1748, from John Reading, ninety acres adjoining the above tract on the west and rear on the line of Thomas Bryerly Esq.

Adam Hall and wife, by deed bearing date Dec. 16. 1742, conveyed to Ananias Allen, one hundred and sixty-six and two thirds acres of the above mentioned five hundred; and Ananias Allen, by deed bearing date Dec. 13. 1743, coveyed to Michael Heanrie the above mentioned one hundred and sixty-six and two thirds acres, the transaction being witnessed by John Smith and George Reading, and acknowledged by John Reading.

Michael Heanrie, by deed bearing date Apr. 6, 1752, conveyed these lands to his son Michael Heanrie Jr. Christopher Falconberger, by deed dated Nov. 9, 1752, conveyed to Christian Sharpenstein two hundred and eleven acres, being the lower portion of his tract; it being the same land which Mr. Sharpenstein conveyed to Jonathan Robins, and which is now owned by William N. Creveling and the heirs of John S. Robins, with other lands. Hannah Heanrie, by deed of trust bearing date Oct. 19, 1757, conveyed to Michael Heanrie, of Readington, and William Bishop of Greenwich, six hundred and ninety-six acres of land in Greenwich township, and one hundred and thirty-two acres in Bethlehem township, to be held in trust for her children until they arrived at the age of twenty-one years, viz: Arthur, Michael, Nathaniel, Elisabeth, and Sarah Heanrie; being the lands fronting on the Musconetcong creek below Bloomsbury, to the westerly line of John Cline's farm, and thence across to the Pohatcong and along Robert I. Smith's and William J. Smith's land to a white oak sapling on the north side of the Musconetcong creek by a spring. This deed was witnessed by Philip Chapman and William Knowles, and acknowledged by Jonathan Petit. A deed for fifty acres was made by Christian Sharpenstein in 1790, which was witnessed by Philip Fonger, Robert Sproull, and John D. Jaques. Adam Runkle Jr. owned lands near Kennedy's mill in Greenwich township.

A deed was made in 1772, in Greenwich township, by Michael Heanrie to Conrad Settle and included lands now occupied by R. H. Kennedy. This transaction was witnessed by Robert Calnett and Charles Hoff. There was a deed made in 1794, for ten acres, by Robert Kennedy and Elisabeth his wife to Peter Fishbach. The property is now owned by Robert I. Smith. This transaction was witnessed by Jacob Eichman and Enoch Kennedy. There was a deed made in 1777 by Conrad Settle to Robert Kennedy, which land is now occupied by R. H.

Kennedy. This transaction was witnessed by Jacob Welsh and Jesse Barber. Capt. Arthur Heanrie's homestead farm is now occupied by H. R. Kennedy. It was bounded on the east by lands of Capt. Benjamin McCullough. Capt. McCullough built the house now occupied by Jesse J. Lake. He owned the lands now in the possession of Robert I. Smith, William J. Smith, John Peter, and the farm on which William Sherrer lives. There was a deed made in 1763 by Capt. McCullough to Samuel Severns, it being the mill property known as Kennedy's Mill. The witnesses to this transaction were Robert Johnston and Patrick McDeed.

Thus we find that the lands on the north as well as on the south side of the Musconetcong have been for generations in the hands of those who were, as a rule, inclined to the Presbyterian faith. Having thus before our minds the section of country in general occupied by the congregation, we may turn to notice more particularly the village of Bloomsbury where the church building is located. This is situated near where the New Brunswick turnpike crosses the Musconetcong creek from Warren into Hunterdon county, and where roads diverge to Pittstown and Little York. The latter of these roads was opened for travel in 1815. "The road from Bloomsbury to Pittstown, a distance of ten miles, is a part of the old one known as 'the Kings Highway', and was originally the dividing line between Bethlehem and Alexandria townships, so far as it crosses Bethlehem. That small portion of Bethlehem west of this road was subsequently taken from Alexandria and added to Bethlehem. The road does not cross a stream between Bloomsbury and Pittstown, though there are many springs and creeks on either side of it." *His. Hun. Co.*, 1881, *p.* 459.

The church is located on the east side of this road a few hundred yards south of where it diverges from the New Brunswick turnpike.

"The name [of the village] is derived from the Bloom family, who were influential here in the early history of the place and at present represented in other localities. It was previously known as Johnson's Iron Works, from Robert Johnson's furnace, which was on the Warren county side of the creek, near where the old charcoal house now stands. Johnson carried on business here as early as 1750. The ore was carted from the south side of the Musconetcong mountain and made into what is known as blooms, and some entertain the idea that the name Bloomsbury originated from this." "The village is beautifully situated at the foot of the Musconetcong mountains, at the lower end of the valley. A small part lies on the north side of the creek, in Warren county." "The site of the village was owned as early as 1810 by George Beidleman of Easton. His son William lived here, having charge of the estate, and the property became his by heirship. His house was on the corner of Bridge Street and Little York road, where Henry Gardner's residence now stands. Mr. Beidleman died here about 1838. His widow still lives in the village [and is a member of the Presbyterian church, Oct. 1883.]" [As to the property here referred to, another authority says it was controlled by Henry Jones and Henry Cortright, sons-in-law of George Beidleman. Subsequently the title vested in Henry Jones. Still later the property was owned by Enoch Green, another son-in-law of George Beidleman, and was controlled by his brother-in-law William Beidleman.] "The next owner of the Bloomsbury property was Henry Jones, who was a distiller and built a still house on the site now occupied by Hoffman's saw mill, below the grist mill. This was the pioneer distillery. He died about 1828. The house in which he lived is now occupied by Theodore Melick. In 1832 his widow built the house where widow Beidleman now lives, [on the southwest corner of Little York road and the road leading to Pittstown, or south across the road from where her husband lived and died.]"

"As late as 1832 the land now occupied by Bloomsbury was a farm, and there were but five houses upon the Bethlehem side of the creek; the old log house that stood where the brick store now is; the old Beidleman·house on the corner where Gardner's house stands; the old yellow house down the York road; and the two log houses of John L. and Bartholomew Lott. These are all standing except the first named. This was kept for several years as a tavern by Charles Tomlinson, and was the first on the south side of the creek." *His. Hun. Co. p. 461.*

Another authority says the property was bought by Joseph Cougle and by him converted into a tavern which was kept by himself.

As to educational advantages it may be said the people of this community enjoyed the common advantages of the times in which they lived. These consisted, in the earlier days, of private schools, and more recently of the common school system of the State. With reference to the religious training of the community it may be said they have never been without it. Even before the sainted David Brainerd came, to a neighboring locality in 1744, as a missionary to the Indians, with whom the whites occupied the land, missionaries had visited the region, preached to the people and founded churches.

"'There came before the Presbytery of New Brunswick, then met at a place now called Lawrenceville,' says the quaint record, 'a supplication for supplies of preaching in Mr. Barber's neighborhood, near Musconnekunk (Musconetcong); and Mr. Cross and Mr. McCrea were directed to supply certain Sabbaths at Lamingtunk (Lamington), and Mr. Barber's.' This Mr. Barber was probably the ancestor of Jesse Barber, father of Phineas, formerly an elder in this (Mansfield) [Washington] church. Subsequent records make it certain that Mr. Barber's neighborhood was identical with parts of old Mansfield and Greenwich; for mention is often made of supplies being sent to Mr. Barber's and Mr. Green's. The former—Mr. Barber's neighborhood—seems to have given place on the records to 'Mansfield Woodhouse' whilst the latter—Mr. Green's—changes on the record to Green's-ridge—Greenidge—Greenage—and at last lower Greenwich." "Greenwich upon Delaware was the district now occupied by Belvidere, Oxford, and part of Harmony." "It is possible that the first Presbyterian houses of worship erected within our bounds, were those of Greenwich and 'Mansfield Woodhouse.' Which was the first erection it is impossible to say. But it is pretty certain that the first meeting house in Greenwich was erected between the years 1739 and 1744; for in the journal of that man of God, David Brainerd, he mentions having preached in Greenwich twice on Sabbath December 9. 1744; and when it is considered that this first log church was so far decayed in 1775 as to render another building necessary, we may infer that it was in the first old church that he preached." *Fiftieth Anniversary of Newton Presbytery, by Rev. D. X. Junkin, D.D., p. 25.*

The three points, then, were Oxford First, near Belvidere; Mansfield Woodhouse, (which stood on the southern slope of the Pohatcong range which divides the Musconetcong and Pohatcong valleys, at the old burying ground adjoining the Washington, N. J., cemetery—which field is now occupied by the First Mansfield (Washington), Musconetcong Valley, and Asbury churches); and Greenwich. If the old log church first erected in Greenwich, on the south side of the Pohatcong creek, one half or three fourths of a mile to the south or southwest of the present church, were still standing, it would probably be in full view, a mile and a half westward, from the site of the present Bloomsbury church.

In that old log church, in 1764, Rev. John Rosbrugh was ordained to the gospel ministry and became, as far as known, the first pastor of the church. The Bloomsbury district was part of that charge and under his ministry, and that of his successors, Rev. Joseph Treat (1775—1797), Rev. William B. Sloan (1798—1834), Rev. David X. Junkin, D.D. (1835 —1851), and Rev. Aaron H. Hand, D.D., the people were always provided with the means of grace.

Thirty-five or thirty-six years before the organization of the Presbyterian church of Bloomsbury, the Methodists commenced to work the field. It seems a circuit preacher visited the place about 1821 and held services in John Pippenger's house, where Samuel Stamets now lives. "Rev. Samuel Hull and Rev. Jacob Hevener preached in the village occasionally about this time. Rev. Seely Bloomer is known to have preached at Daniel Stires' residence, then standing near the Central Railroad arch. Willever's and Stiers' houses became the headquarters of the Methodist preachers when in the place." "In 1835 a suitable place for public service was purchased. It was the property now owned by Joseph B. Boss, and occupied as a double dwelling, near the corner north of the church. It was originally a cabinet shop belonging to a

Mr. Helmsman, and later a wheelwright shop. [Another authority says the building was originally built by Mrs. Nancy Jones for her son George, to be occupied as a wheelwright shop.] Henry Willever and Daniel Stires were among the early members, and contributed largely to the establishment of the infant church. When Mr. Willever died, in 1841, he bequeathed $400 to the society, with which to refit the wheelwright shop and adapt it to church purposes. While this was being done Rev. Mr. Page and his colaborer Rev. J. P. Daly, preached in the school house. A Rev. Mr. Chattels preached the dedicatory sermon; he was appointed to this circuit about 1839." *His. Hun. Co., p. 462.*

We find then that the Methodists had been occupying and actively cultivating the field for more than twenty years before the Presbyterians organized a church. Thus we have before us some of the circumstances which surrounded the people of the community prior to the organization of the First Presbyterian Church of Bloomsbury, and which exerted their influence in directing the current of its affairs.

CHAPTER II.
ERECTION OF A CHURCH BUILDING AND FIRST PASTORATE UNDER REV. W. E. WESTERVELT.

Organization talked of prior to 1834, during pastorate of Rev. Wm. B. Sloan at Greenwich. Also under pastorate of Rev. D. X. Junkin, 1835—1851. Definite action taken relative thereto under pastorate of Rev. A. H. Hand. Church organized 1857. Causes which made organization necessary. Services in school house. Incorporation. Donation of site for church building. Calling of first pastor. Organization of choir. Outpost at Bethlehem. Erection and dedication of church edifice. Building injured by storm. Districting of the congregation. Resignation of first pastor.

As we have seen, the field occupied by the First Presbyterian Church of Bloomsbury was originally included in the bounds of the old historic Greenwich church, Warren county, New Jersey. As the facts relative to the early history of that church may be found in a discourse delivered at its Centenary, on the present site; in a discourse commemorative of the first half century of the Presbytery of Newton, by Rev. David X. Junkin, D.D.; and in "Rosbrugh," by the author of this sketch, it is unnecessary to give, further than we have already done, a retrospect of the religious characteristics of the community prior to the formation of the Bloomsbury church.

As early as during the pastorate of Rev. William B. Sloan in Greenwich church, which closed in 1834, the formation of a church at Bloomsbury was talked of. During the pastorate of Rev. David X. Junkin, D.D., from 1835—1851, the matter was spoken of from time to time but no definite action was taken. During the early part of the pastorate of Rev. Aaron H. Hand, D.D., commencing in 1851, the question seems to have received little or no attention. But in 1857 the subject assumed a practical aspect, so far as the Greenwich church was concerned. In the Centenary discourse above referred to, p. 41, Dr. Junkin says: "In November, 1858 [1857], the Bloomsbury church was organized of persons belonging to this church, for which purpose forty-one were dismissed." The need of a Presbyterian church at this point was occasioned, at least in part, by the impetus which the place received from the extension of the New Jersey Central Railroad through the Musconetcong valley, to Easton, Pennsylvania. This occurred in 1852. So great was the increase of population and resources at this point that it was felt to be a question, not simply of practicability, but of necessity that a congregation be organized and a church building erected in the locality to accommodate the forty or more Presbyterian families who were residents of the village and its immediate vicinity. The initiatory step seems to have been taken by William J. Smith, who, some time in August, 1857, spoke of the matter to Henry R. Kennedy. A week or so subsequent to this there met, informally, under the trees at the residence of Robert I. Smith on the north side of the Musconetcong creek, the following gentlemen, viz: James Bird, Henry Gardner Sr., David F. Wean, Henry R. Kennedy, William S. Gardner, Robert I. Smith, and William J. Smith, who discussed the subject and resolved to attempt some practical results. The question received a practical solution when on Sep. 1, 1857, the friends of the enterprise founded the church. The following subscription paper was circulated, viz:

"We, the signers hereunto, feeling the necessity of having a convenient house of worship in our village, agree to pay the sums affixed to our names toward the erection of a church edifice for the worship of Almighty God, to be located within the bounds of the village of Bloomsbury; provided that said church edifice shall be owned and occupied by a congregation hereafter to be organized to be entitled and called the First Presbyterian Church of Bloomsbury. Said congregation shall elect officers and call a pastor to preside over and minister unto said church and congregation, and shall enjoy all the immunities and privileges granted and allotted to such churches and congregations according to the forms and usages of the Presbyterian church."

The following names are found attached to this paper, viz: Henry Gardner, Robert H. Kennedy, James Bird, S. C. Smith, Wm. S. Gardner, John Carter, H. R. Kennedy, Wm. J. Smith, Moses Robins, Joseph Lair, Wm. Tinsman, J. W. Willever, J. Gardner, J. Hance, Wm. S. Hulsizer, Joseph B. Boss, Abram James, Sarah A. Carter, Peter Smith, Jacob Vliet, Hannah Williamson, James J. Willever, Robert I. Smith, J. C. Stewart, Theodore Gardner, Benjamin Parker, Samuel Jeramberger, Charles Petty, John R. Smith, E. T. Vliet, Abram Hance, and David F. Wean. These persons subscribed a sum amounting in the aggregate to $4075.

A petition signed by one hundred and twenty-nine persons was presented to the Newton Presbytery at its meeting, Oct. 6, 1857, by Wm. J. Smith and John T. Bird, asking that the church be organized. The request was granted and the following committee was appointed to carry into effect the wishes of the people, viz: Revs. Hugh N. Wilson, D.D.,

J. Arndt Riley, George C. Bush, with ruling elders Peter Winter, of Harmony, Adam R. Reese, of Phillipsburg, and Philip Muchler, of Asbury. The committee convened in the Methodist Episcopal church of Bloomsbury, on Oct. 29. of that year and attended to the duties of their appointment. The record of the meeting is as follows:

"Certain members of the church of Greenwich, of the Presbytery of Newton, assembled in the Methodist Episcopal church of Bloomsbury for the purpose of organizing a church to be called the 1st Presbyterian Church of Bloomsbury, in pursuance of certain action of said Presbytery by appointing a committee thereunto, whereat the Rev. Doctor Wilson presided, by order of said committee." The following members were received for organization, viz: John T. Bird, Wm. J. Smith, Sarah E. Smith, John R. Smith, Sarah C. Smith, Mary Hulsizer, Nancy Mitchell, Lydia Cochran, Sarah Stiner, Margaret Hance, Thomas Young, Rebecca Ann Young, John Hance, Catharine Hance, Jane R. Smith, Annie Parker, Abram Hance, Susan Housel, Susan McPherson, Penelope McPherson, Deborah Young, Peter Hart, Mary Hart, Annie Creveling, Henry Gardner, Elisabeth L. Kennedy, Henry R. Kennedy, Elisabeth Gardner, Miriam K. Kennedy, David F. Wean, Absalom James, Robert I. Smith, Mary H. Smith, Wm. S. Gardner, Rachel Tinsman, Joseph C. Smith, James Bird, Mary Bird, Emily A. Hulsizer, Abram W. Smith, Wm. S. Hulsizer, and Wm. Tinsman—forty-two in all, among whom were twenty-six heads of families.

The same day James Bird, Henry R. Kennedy, Wm. Tinsman and Wm. J. Smith were elected to the office of ruling elder, and after a recess, in the evening, all (except Mr. Tinsman, who was afterwards ordained) were ordained and installed in their office. The congregation convened in the school house in the village on the tenth day of November of the same year, pursuant to an order of the Presbyterial committee. At this meeting Rev. George C. Bush presided. Upon this date session received Wm. Tinsman by certificate from the Lutheran church and he was ordained and installed an elder. The congregation proceeded to elect John T. Bird, Wm. S. Hulsizer, John Hance, and Robert I. Smith, deacons. All but the last two were accordingly set apart to that office. At the same time Wm. S. Gardner, Abram Hance, and Joseph W. Willever were elected trustees. These trustees, under date of Nov. 16. 1857, signed and sealed their declaration of the corporate existence of the "First Presbyterian Church of Bloomsbury," in the following form, viz:

"Whereas a meeting was held on the tenth day of November, A. D. 1857, by the congregation hereinafter to be named, for the purpose of electing trustees of said congregation, at least ten days previous notice of such meeting having been given by an advertisement in open view at the place of such meeting, we, Willam S Gardner, Abram Hance, and Joseph W. Willever being elected trustees by a plurality of votes of such of the said congregation as were present, we do hereby certify that we have taken upon ourselves the name of 'The First Presbyterian Church of Bloomsbury.' Given under our hands and seals this six-teenth day of November, in the year of our Lord one thousand eight hundred and fifty-seven."

(Signed.)   W. S. Gardner. .   SEAL.
                      Abram Hance.   SEAL.
                      Joseph W. Willever.   SEAL.

This document was duly recorded Nov. 17. in Hunterdon county records, where it may be found, Special Deeds Folio, vol. 111, pp. 376, 377.

Following immediately upon this, Mr. Adam D. Runkle donated a suitable piece of land to the congregation upon which to erect a house of worship, deeding the same over to them under date of Nov. 19. 1857.

On Dec. 10. 1857, session received a letter from Rev. Sidney G. Law, of Brooklyn (formerly of Iowa), asking for an opportunity to preach to the people as a candidate for the pastoral office in the congregation. Jan. 19. 1858, session directed that he be invited to visit the congregation, which he did, preaching two Sabbaths and delivering a week day lecture. At the same time, Jan. 19. action was taken with reference to seeking supplies from the theological seminaries at Princeton and New Brunswick. Jan. 27. a letter was received from Prof. W. Henry Green, of Princeton Seminary, recommending Rev. Frederick A. King, of Rahway, and Rev. W. E. Westervelt, of Patterson, New Jersey. On Feb. 14. session invited both Mr. King and Mr. Westervelt to visit the congregation and preach as candidates. They both came and preached two Sabbaths and delivered a week day lecture. The congregation now authorized the session to call a meeting for the election of a pastor. Messrs. H. R. Kennedy and Wm. Tinsman were appointed a committee to invite Rev. Messrs. George C. Bush and James Lewers to assist in the contemplated election. This committee reported on March 4. that Mr. Bush was absent from home, whereupon Rev. J. Y. Mitchell and Dr. A. H. Hand were invited to attend. The congregation convened in the school house on March 3. 1858, for the purpose of taking steps for the election of a pastor. It was decided that a meeting for this purpose should be held on the 6. of March. The congregation accordingly convened on March 6. 1858. Rev. J. Y. Mitchell, of Phillipsburg, presided, being assisted by Rev. A. H. Hand, D.D., of Greenwich, who offered prayer after the singing of a hymn. A sermon was preached by Mr. Mitchell, after which the election was entered into. The choice fell upon Mr. W. E. Westervelt, a licentiate of the Presbytery of Passaic. The meeting directed that the call be signed by a special committe consisting of the following persons, viz: Henry Gardner, Sr., Adam D. Runkle, and Robert H. Kennedy. Mr. Mitchell was authorized to notify Mr. Westervelt of his election.

At a meeting held March 22. the congregation appointed Messrs. Wm. Tinsman and Spencer C. Smith commissioners to prosecute the call for the newly elected pastor before Presbytery. The commissioners accordingly appeared in Presbytery, Apr. 6. at the Musconetcong Valley Church, and presented the call for Mr. Westervelt's services. The same being found in order was placed in his hands and accepted by him. Presbytery thereupon appointed a committee to arrange for the examination, ordination, and installation of Mr. Westervelt, who made the following report, viz: the time to be Apr. 15. ensuing; the Moderator, Rev. Henry Reeves, of Belvidere, to preside and propose the constitutional questions; Rev. W. C. Cattell to preach the sermon; Rev. Dr. Hugh Wilson, of Hackettstown, to charge the pastor; and Rev. George C. Bush, of Stewartsville, to charge the people. The trial sermon was to be founded upon Rom. 5 : 1. The Presbytery accordingly met in the Methodist Episcopal church of Bloomsbury at the time appointed, at 10 o'clock, A. M., and was called to order by Rev. George C. Bush, the last Moderator present. Mr. Westervelt was examined in the forenoon, and at 2 o'clock in the afternoon the ordination services took place. In the absence of Rev. Mr. Reeves, Dr. A. H. Hand presided, proposed the constitutional questions and offered the ordaining prayer; Rev. W. C. Cattell preached the sermon; and Rev. S. McNair, of Washington, gave the charge to the pastor; and Rev. George C. Bush gave the charge to the people.

Mr. Westervelt having been thus installed on Apr. 15, 1858, went forward with his work among the people. At a meeting of session held June 13. 1858, the question of making Jugtown a preaching point was discussed, and the pastor was instructed to write to Rev. James Lewers, of Asbury, and inquire if such step would be regarded by him as an encroachment upon his field of labor. At this meeting it was formally decided that the singing in the church should be under the control of the session. The pastor was requested to draw up a set of rules and regulations for the government of the singing. This he did, reporting the same Jun. 18. They are as follows:

"Impressed with the importance of having our church music conducted in a manner that will be in keeping with its acknowledged sacred character, and that will be best adapted to the spiritual edification of all; and moreover, wishing to avoid if possible, those serious evils which so generally are connected with this part of divine worship; we, the session of the First Presbyterian Church of Bloomsbury do unanimously adopt the following resolutions and regulations, viz:

Resolved I. That the music of this church be under the immediate supervision and control of its session.

Resolved II. That the performer on the instrument be selected from among the members of the congregation. [Player has had no salary.]

Resolved III. That the singing shall be conducted by a choir, which shall be subject to the following regulations, viz:

1. The number of members constituting the choir shall be limited to twelve. (Changed to fifteen Sep. 6.)

2. No one shall be a member of the choir who is not a regular member of the congregation.

3. Every member of the choir is expected to perform regularly his or her part of the duties of the choir.

4. The tunes sung during service shall be taken from collections of music approved by the session.

5. If set pieces of music, sung or played previous to or at the opening of the service, they shall either be taken from collections specified in Reg. 4., or else they shall have previously received the approval of session.

6. The practice of singing or performing on the instrument while the congregation are retiring from the house, is prohibited.

7. Not more than one new tune shall be introduced on each Sabbath.

8. Members of the choir have no right to invite others, not members, to take seats with them in the choir.

9. On special occasions the choir may, with the concurrence of the session, invite some other choir, or specified number of experienced singers to unite with and assist them.

10. Seats shall be assigned to the different members of the choir by its leader; and there shall be no changing of seats without his permission.

11. The above regulations shall be signed by the several members of the choir.

The deacons were also authorized to have charge of the collections in the church, not only for the poor but also for all benevolent objects. Aug. 1. session received information from Mr. Lewers that there would be no objection to the occupying of the school house at Jugtown by the Bloomsbury congregation one Sabbath in four weeks. Accordingly that day, Aug. 1., services were commenced at that point. It was arranged that there should be a prayer meeting at Bloomsbury at such times as the pastor was absent holding services at Jugtown, the second service at Bloomsbury at this time being held in the afternoon.

Up to this time the people had been holding their services in the public school house, and were at the same time busily engaged in the erection of their new church building. It was now rapidly approaching completion. It is a commodious frame structure, 44 by 68 feet, neatly finished and furnished, with a seating capacity of 700. Galleries extend around three sides of the room. From bills on record it would seem the building cost the following sums, viz:

Basement	$796.71
Superstructure—by A. R. Dilts	4638.10
Furnishing	148.29
Total	$5583.10

On the 6. of September the subject of the dedication of the new church was taken up. The time fixed upon as the commencement of these exercises was Oct. 7., at 10 o'clock A. M. There were to be two services a day for four days, viz: Thursday, Friday, Saturday and Sabbath. On Sabbath the sacrament of the Lord's supper was to be administered. Rev. D. X. Junkin, D.D., of Holidaysburg, Penn., was chosen to preach the dedicatory sermon. The selection of persons to officiate at the other services was left to the pastor of the church. It was decided to invite to these services the ministers and congregations of the Newton Presbytery, together with the following ministers and congregations, viz: Rev. Messrs. Coleman, Plit, Conkling, Hinkle, Williamson and McNair.

At this meeting (Sep. 6.) Mrs. H. R. Kennedy was elected organist. Mr. John T. Bird, the leader of the choir, having removed from the congregation, resigned his position and Robert I. Smith was appointed to fill the same. The Moderator was requested to meet with the choir and fix upon some book of Psalmody to be used in the congregation. The choice made was that of the Old School branch of the church.

On Oct. 3., in order to suit the convenience of Dr. Junkin, the time for the dedicatory services of the church was changed from the 7. to the 14. inst. These services accordingly took place at this time substantially as arranged on the 6, of Sept. previous. Upon that day a collection was taken up amounting to $104.09. On Oct. 16. Dr. Junkin was requested to furnish a copy of his dedicatory sermon for publication. It was also decided at this time that the expenses of delegates from the congregation to Synod should be borne by the congregation.

The people had now become possessed of a suitable place in which to hold their services. In anticipation of the future needs of the congregation they had also, during the year 1858, purchased a piece of ground adjoining that donated by Mr. Runkle as a site for a church building.

Whilst seeming to be prospered they were soon to be called upon to lament a discouraging calamity which befel their building. A terrific storm swept through the valley which blew down the steeple, cracked the bell, and otherwise injured the structure. The people however soon set to work to repair the damage. On Feb. 9. 1859, a meeting of the congregation was held at which it was decided to "repair the church immediately beginning from the foundation up." The work was to be done by contract and the money therefor was to be raised by subscription. Messrs. S. C. Smith and John Hance were added to a committee of the trustees to superintend the work. Messrs. Wm. J. Smith, S. C. Smith, John Carter, James Stewart, Rev. Wm. E. Westervelt, Henry Gardner, Sr., Thomas Young, Joseph C. Smith, John R. Smith and Wm. Tinsman were appointed a committee to solicit contributions from the different churches to meet the expenses of these repairs. At the same time Messrs. Robert I. Smith and H. R. Kennedy were appointed a committee to procure a bell. The work here referred to was done by the Kellars, of Easton, Penn. James Gardner was an active and leading participant on the part of the congregation, in securing a reparation of the injury sustained by the building. Wm. Chapman, of Chapman's Quarries, Northampton county, Penn., from whom had been purchased the original roof, now donated slate for a new roof and had the same put on at his own expense.

Nov. 1. 1859, the hour of the second service, which had been in the afternoon, was changed to evening. At this time the question of making Garrison's school house, on Musconetcong mountain, a preaching point was discussed, but no definite action taken relative thereto. The question was discussed of dividing the congregation into districts to be under the supervision of the different members of session for a given time, during which they were to visit the families assigned to them and at the end of the specified time report to session. Decision upon the matter was deferred until after the pastor should preach on the subject of the duties of ruling elders. The question of securing a better attendance upon the prayer meeting was discussed: also that of having a sessional conference and prayer meeting statedly. This met with approval of all, but definite action thereon was deferred to a future meeting.

On May 14. 1860, the question of dividing up the congregation into districts was again taken up. The following division was made, viz: "To Mr. Tinsman were assigned all the families on the south side of the Musconetcong creek and east of Mrs. Widow Boss' place, whose house is the starting point; to Mr. Bird were assigned all the families on the same side of the creek westward from his own house, as far as church street, with three families on it; to Mr. Kennedy were assigned all the families on the north side of the creek; and to Mr. Smith those on the south side westward from church street and southward from Alexandria street to the uttermost bounds of the congregation, excepting the families of Messrs. John R. Smith and Peter R. Smith." It was now decided that the pastor should preach on the subject of the duties of ruling elders, on Sabbath, May 27., and at that time acquaint the people with the action of session as to districting the congregation.

Oct. 14. 1860, Mrs. H. R. Kennedy resigned the position of organist and Miss Mary Smith was appointed to fill the vacancy.

Mr. Westervelt having expressed his desire to resign the pastoral charge of the congregation, a special meeting of Presbytery was held at Bloomsbury, July 2. 1861. After hearing Mr. Westervelt, and Spencer C. Smith, the commissioner from the congregation, the pastoral relation was dissolved. The church was granted leave to supply its own pulpit, and Rev. Mr. Tully was appointed to declare the pulpit vacant, on the succeeding Sabbath. During the pastorate of Mr. Westervelt forty-one persons had been received into the church, sixteen on profession and twenty-five by certificate. These with the forty-two who came in at the organization, made a membership of eighty-three, Jan. 13. 1861. Seven couples had been married and nineteen infants had been baptized.

CHAPTER III.

PRELIMINARIES TO REUNION. PASTORATE OF REV. MR. VAN DYKE.

Calling of second pastor. Church transferred from Newton to Raritan Presbytery. Revival of 1861. *Sabbath school work. Dissensions. Outposts at Garrison's, Bethlehem and Franklin school houses. Election of additional elder and deacons. Reunion. Pastor's salary increased. Church injured by lightning. Resignation of second pastor.*

On July 7. 1861, session invited Mr. Joseph S. VanDyke, a licentiate of the Presbytery of Elisabethtown, to preach the next Sabbath as a candidate for the pastoral office in the congregation, with the understanding that subsequent opportunity to preach would be afforded by session. This invitation was accordingly accepted by Mr. VanDyke. On July 21. he was invited again to preach as a candidate on two succeeding Sabbaths, which invitation he also accepted. On Aug. 4. session received two petitions of like import signed by one hundred and thirty-six members and supporters of the church, requesting them to call a meeting for the election of a pastor. The request was granted and the time for the meeting was fixed for Tuesday. Aug. 6., at 2 o'clock P. M. Elders James Bird and Wm. Tinsman were appointed a committee to invite Rev. George C. Bush to preside at the meeting. The congregation accordingly met on Aug. 6., Mr. Bush presiding, at which time Mr. VanDyke was elected pastor, on a salary of $650, payable semiannually. The call was signed by all the officers of the church present and attested by the moderator and secretary of the meeting.

On Aug. 24., the question of holding services at Hawk's school house was discussed and elder Smith was appointed to accompany the pastor elect to that point to ascertain if such service was desirable.

Sep. 26. in accordance with action previously taken in congregational meeting, session recorded the appointment of S. C. Smith and Daniel Williamson as commissioners to prosecute the call for Mr. VanDyke before the Presbytery. These gentlemen accordingly appeared in Presbytery and performed the duty assigned them. Oct. 10. Mr. VanDyke preached his ordination sermon and was installed pastor of the church.

In 1861 the Bloomsbury church, with others, was transferred from the Presbytery of Newton to that of Raritan. In December of this year there was considerable religious interest manifested in the congregation, and on the 14. and 15. of that month, twenty-two of the young people were admitted to church membership by profession of their faith in Christ, besides others by certificate. A series of special services was arranged and neighboring ministers invited to assist in the same. Dec. 28. a meeting of session was held at which two questions were considered, viz: "1. To consider the propriety of having a meeting of session for the purpose of receiving to church membership those desirous of applying with a view of making their public profession at our next communion. 2. To consider the propriety of granting the privilege of communing with the Greenwich church to-morrow, to such new converts as shall have passed the session and desire it." The session decided to hold a meeting for the examination of applicants, but did not accord to them the privilege of communing at Greenwich before making a public profession of their faith. Session accordingly met Jan. 3. 1862 and received by profession of faith in Christ, twelve persons, and resolved to continue the series of meetings which had been in progress up to this time. It was also resolved that a special communion season be observed on the first Sabbath of February. On Feb. 1. and 2. five were received by profession and five by certificate.

March 20. 1862, the congregation elected Theodore Gardner, Joseph C. Smith and Wm. Vliet trustees. March 23. it was decided that the sacrament of the Lord's supper should be administered four times a year, viz: on second Sabbath of February, May, August and November.

May 11. the subject of the Sabbath school was discussed and the pastor was requested, at his convenience, to enlighten the congregation as to its wants and their duty in relation thereto.

Aug. 10. the subject of petitioning Synod to return the church from the care of the Raritan to its former relations with the Presbytery of Newton was discussed, and Sep. 28. it was decided to convene the congregation to obtain an expression of their opinion in the matter. The congregational meeting was held Oct. 11. 1862, at which time it was decided to remain in connection with the Presbytery of Raritan.

Notwithstanding there had been in past, evidences of the Holy Spirit's presence among the people, it soon became manifest that the Evil one was also busy. Dissensions arose which distracted the church and impeded the progress of the work. A number absented themselves from the ordinances and in other respects manifested their indisposition to cooperate with the church in its work. The matter became so flagrant as to demand the official consideration of it by the session. Accordingly at a meeting of session held Jan. 24. 1864, "The pastor made a statement of the unhappy dissensions in the church, and proposed that a committee of the session be appointed to visit those who by their absence from the stated ordinances and services of the church have seemed to be alienated in feeling. After serious discussion the measure was approved, and session entertained the hope that through the guidings of the providence of God this course prayerfully pursued will

8 *First Presbyterian Church of Bloomsbury.*

bring about reconciliation and peace in our beloved Zion. The pastor with elders Bird and Tinsman were appointed on this committee. The committee reported Oct. 14. that "In most cases they found cause for encouragement and believe that they will return to their duty in the church, but in one case they entertain no hope of return."

Notwithstanding the discouraging aspect of affairs in the congregation, the work of carrying the truth to those who were on the outskirts was not neglected. March 27, 1864. it was decided that preaching services should be held thereafter every fourth Sabbath alternately at Garrison's, Bethlehem and Franklin school houses. At the latter place the attendance was large and interesting and indicative of good in the future. On this account the second service at the church was to be held only once a month. At this time the pastor reported favorably of the attendance at the outposts and that the prospects of the church were brightening. It was thus made manifest that the judicious use of the means of grace had not been without effect in correcting some of the evils existing in the congregation.

Apr. 1. 1866, it was arranged to hold a congregational meeting on Apr. 14. for the purpose of electing one elder, five trustees and two deacons. The meeting was held according to appointment, at which time Henry V. Brittain was elected elder; Charles E. Williamson, Moses Robins and Charles Petty, deacons; Wm. Vliet, Abram Hance, Joseph W. Willever, Theodore Gardner, Robert I. Smith, Daniel Williamson and Wm Welsh, trustees. It was decided to ordain the elder and deacons elect the ensuing Sabbath.

In the latter part of 1866 the officers of the church felt the importance of arousing the people to a greater activity and more unreserved consecration to the Master's work. Accordingly on Nov. 11. 1866, it was arranged to hold a sessional prayer meeting on the first Sabbath of each month, and a communicants prayer meeting each Sabbath previous to communion. Whilst thus looking after the internal welfare of the congregation the session was not blind to the great interests of Zion in general. At this time the question of reunion of the two branches of the church was claiming the attention of the people. To show their interest in the matter the session, on Sep. 22. 1867, instructed its delegate to Synod to support Synodical action looking to the reunion of the Presbyterian church, and thus revealed its attitude toward the great result which was consummated in 1870.

At the close of this year the people took commendable action in the matter of the pastor's salary, as will be seen by the following record:

"Bloomsbury, Dec. 28. 1867. Whereas the Presbytery of Raritan at its late meeting passed a resolution requesting the officers of our churches to inquire into the sufficiency of the salaries of the pastors of our churches, the congregation of the First Church of Bloomsbury being called for such purpose by request of the officers, who having inquired into the case of our pastor, the Rev. Joseph S. VanDyke, have found such to be the case in regard to our pastor. Accordingly a meeting was called for the purpose of raising the pastor's salary. Said meeting appointed a committee of five persons (trustees of the church) to assess the pews of our church to raise the present salary to one thousand dollars. Accordingly the pews were assessed to raise that amount."

Following upon the increasing of the pastor's salary, the people were called upon to meet an additional expense. This arose from the church needing repairs as seen from the following record. viz:

"Bloomsbury, March 28. 1868. In pursuance of regular notice, a congregational meeting was held in this church, organized by appointing Wm. J. Smith, president, and Henry R. Kennedy, secretary. The following preamble and resolutions were adopted:

Whereas the steeple and other parts of our church need repairs, therefore

Resolved that the trustees be and hereby are empowered to repaint and repair the church as they deem necessary, the expenditure therefor not to exceed three hundred dollars."

"The present board of trustees was unanimously reelected for the ensuing term of one year."

At a meeting duly called on May 1. 1869, the congregation united with the pastor in asking the Presbytery of Raritan to dissolve the pas-

toral relation existing between him and them that he might accept a
call to the Second Presbyterian Church of Cranbury, N. J.

Daniel Williamson and Wm. Tinsman were appointed commissioners
to communicate the action of the church to the Presbytery. The Presbytery dissolved the pastoral relation May 4, 1869. During this pastorate of a little more than seven years and a half, there were received into the church one hundred and seventeen persons, seventy-three by
profession of their faith in Christ, and forty-four by certificate. There
were united in marriage thirty-eight couples, and twenty-nine children
were baptized. Under Mr. VanDyke's ministry the matter of church
discipline was not neglected; seven cases were taken up and disposed of.

CHAPTER IV.

PASTORATE OF REV. MR. SCOTT. BUILDING OF PARSONAGE.

*Parsonage. Sacramental occasions. Call of third pastor. Congregation re-
districted. Revival of 1870. Outpost work declining. Congregational rules.
Church returns to Newton Presbytery. Reunion. Memorial fund. Pastor's
salary increased. John P. Smith legacy. Sexton's duties. Storm injures church.*

At the close of Mr. VanDyke's pastorate it became manifest to the
congregation that the erection of a parsonage was essential to the prosperity of the church. It was found that with the amount of salary
which the people felt able to pay, the pastor could not rent a house,
maintain his family and at the same time devote himself to the pastoral work with that efficiency which the circumstances of the case seemed

to require. Accordingly at the meeting of the congregation May 1. the following action was taken relative to the building of a parsonage:

"*Whereas* the people of this church and congregation have long felt the importance of possessing a parsonage, and in the early period of the organization of this church, a piece of ground was purchased for such building, and

Whereas certain members of this church have voluntarily gone amidst the congregation and submitted the matter to respective heads of families with a view to obtain their opinion, and if favorable, to solicit subscriptions toward the immediate erection of such edifice, and

Whereas the unanimous sentiment is favorable, and liberal donations have been subscribed and assured, amounting to about $1850, and other gentlemen of the congregation and neighborhood having expressed a determination to give when the building shall be in a state of progress, therefore it is

Resolved that a building committee be appointed and the work commenced immediately."

The building committee appointed consisted of Messrs. John Peters and Moses Robins. As we have intimated, the people had secured by purchase from Mr. Adam Runkle, in 1858, a lot of ground adjoining that donated by him for the site of the church building. Upon this piece of ground, which lay directly south of the church lot, the parsonage was erected. After a few unimportant additions and changes, it furnishes a commodious and comfortable home for the pastor of the church, being 22 by 59 feet, ground plan, and containing twelve apartments exclusive of halls, pantries, attics &c. A congregational meeting was held Nov. 9. 1869, at which time the committee appointed May 1. of that year, to build the parsonage, made the following report, viz:

Contract price	$2200.00
Extras	42.25
Labor and material by congregation not included	243.28
Total	$2485.53

Amount on subscription, paid and unpaid	$2003.00
Balance due and unpaid	482.53
Total	$2485.53

The committee in charge was continued to collect the balance of the subscriptions, after which the trustees were authorized to assume the remainder of the indebtedness. The thanks of the congregation having been bestowed upon the committee who built the parsonage, attention was immediately turned, at this meeting, Nov. 9., to the matter of erecting a barn for the use of the pastors. In the interest of this object Henry R. Kennedy purchased a lot from the New Jersey Central R. R. Co., which adjoined the church lot on the north and which fronted on the centre street of the village. This he donated to the congregation, and in due time the desired building was erected thereon.

During the vacancy succeeding Mr. VanDyke's pastorate, a number of ministers preached for the people, among whom we find the names of Rev. Messrs. Jameson, Kugler, Dole, Dernelle, Simonson, Grant, Carrol and Scott. The session decided, June 5. 1869, to invite three of these ministers to preach three successive Sabbaths, as candidates, commencing June 13. The ministers to be invited were Rev. Messrs. John Simonson, Daniel Dernelle and A. G. Dole.

July 11. the times of observing the sacrament of the Lord's supper were changed from the second Sabbath in February, May, August and November respectively, to the second Sabbath in May, September and January, thus having three sacramental occasions instead of four. At this time record was made of the fact that the above named clergymen had preached to the congregation as arranged, including also Rev. H. B. Scott, who had been informally invited. It was thought the people were ready to elect a pastor, and the session called a congregational meeting, to convene July 17., to take action in the matter. Elder James Bird was appointed a committee to invite Rev. J. B. Kugler to preside on the occasion. The meeting was held as appointed, at which Rev. H. B. Scott was elected pastor.

On August 29. of this year (1869) the congregation was again divided up, as it had been done previously, into districts as follows, viz:

"*Resolved* that all the population located south of the Musconetcong river, and east of the north and south avenue, including the families of George W. Race and Charles Petit, be confided to the care of elder Wm. Tinsman; all the population located south of Bird street and east of Church street (in the village of Bloomsbury), be confided to the care of elder James Bird; all the population located north of Bird street and west of Church street, be confided to the care of elder Wm. J. Smith; all the population located north of the Musconetcong river, be confided to the care of elder Henry R. Kennedy,"

In the early part of 1870 another manifestation of the especial presence of the Holy Spirit in the congregation was enjoyed. Jan. 8. seven were received on profession of faith, and on the 23. of the same month, thirty-six were admitted A special sacramental occasion was observed on the 30. of the month for the special benefit of those who had been admitted to the church. At the close of the pastorate of Mr. VanDyke it seems the outpost preaching was discontinued. The matter however was discussed again May 7. 1870, at which time Mr. Scott expressed his intention to preach occasionally during the summer, at Garrison's school house.

June 11. 1870, "The trustees elected to serve the church for this year, met this day and were duly organized. The following persons were elected as the annual officers of the board: Mr. Daniel Williamson, president; Mr. Theodore Gardner, secretary; Mr. Robert I. Smith, treasurer. Mr. Abram Hance was appointed a committee to keep the church and parsonage in repair and see that all necessary repairs are promptly attended to &c.; Mr. R. I. Smith, a committee to rent pews and see to the collection of the same." The following rules and by-laws were unanimously adopted:

"The secretary shall keep a strict account of all business; of all money raised and the object for which it has been raised, and the object for which it has been appropriated, and that a strict account in writing shall be annually submitted to the congregation, when a committee shall be appointed to examine and audit the accounts of secretary and treasurer.

"The trustees shall appropriate all moneys to the special object for which said money was raised or collected. No money shall be otherwise appropriated unless by a two thirds vote of the board at its regular meeting.

"In order to meet the wishes of all and remove the objections of some, the following laws were unanimously adopted by the congregation on Feb. 9. 1859, and reaffirmed on Apr. 1. 1870."

RULE I. No pew in the middle aisle shall be rented by halves, or to two families or individuals, when one family desires to rent and occupy the same.

RULE II. That the practice of renting one half pews to communicants of more than three persons in the family be hereafter discontinued, as being an infringement on the rights of fellow communicants.

RULE III. All communicants and all heads of families who are communicants, shall be required to furnish themselves and families with sittings in the church.

RULE IV. Each party renting a pew shall be held responsible for said rent, and no person shall in any case be permitted to sublet or rent any part of said pew.

RULE V. All single persons who are communicants, shall be required to pay for one sitting, unless such are minors or females who are provided with sittings by their parents.

RULE VI. The church is unanimously resolved that the above rules shall be carried out in all cases, and that no change or addition shall be made thereto unless due notice has been given and a regular meeting of the congregation called for the purpose.

In 1870, at the reunion of the two branches of the Presbyterian church, this congregation was again placed under the care of the Presbytery of Newton, the name being placed upon the roll June 22. Dec. 17. it was determined by session to raise $1500 as this congregation's part of the "Memorial Fund" for the consummation of the union between the two branches of the church.

Apr. 8. 1871, at a congregational meeting, "It was on motion decided that the congregation now elect two new trustees to fill the vacancy now in the board, occasioned by the expiration of the term of office of two of the board. The following persons were elected again for the term of six years: Abram Hanee, Joseph W. Willever. It was then on motion decided that we now reelect the whole board, and it was carried unanimously." At a congregational meeting held Jan. 20. 1872, it was decided to increase the pastor's salary to $1200 per annum. In order to meet this additional sum, Henry R. Kennedy, Wm. S. Hulsizer and Joseph C. Smith were appointed a committee to act with the trustees in assessing an amount, not exceeding $200, pro rata upon the pews, except the two front ones in the middle block. The trustees were also instructed to declare vacant any pews on which the full amount of rental was not paid. July 14. 1872, session resolved to maintain a sessional monthly concert of prayer upon the last Saturday of each month.

We find at this period of the church's history that those who were its friends in life did not fail to remember it in death. This is shown by a minute adopted in congregational meeting, Nov. 23. 1872, which is self explanatory and which is as follows:

"*Whereas* at a previous meeting of the congregation held in the church, the board of trustees were appointed a committee to raise a given sum of $1500 in order to secure a legacy left this church in the will of John P. Smith, deceased, asked to be relieved, and move that the elders of the church serve in their stead." This legacy was duly secured by the congregation.

A congregational meeting was held July 20. 1872, for the purpose of electing trustees and attending to other matters of importance. Owing to the fewness of the persons present, the meeting abjourned to meet on the 27. of the same month. The congregation accordingly convened at that time and elected Joseph C. Smith and John S. Carter trustees. At this meeting the following action was taken with reference to the legacy bequeathed to the congregation by John P. Smith, deceased, viz :

"*Whereas* the late John P. Smith, of the township of Greenwich, county of Warren, and state of New Jersey, in his last will and testament did bequeath to the First Presbyterian Church of Bloomsbury, in the county of Hunterdon, state aforesaid, the sum of one thousand dollars upon the condition that the said church raise in actual cash the sum of fifteen hundred dollars within one year after the decease of said donor, John P. Smith, aforesaid, therefore be it

Resolved, that the congregation of the First Presbyterian Church of Bloomsbury having been duly called to meet on this 27. day of July, 1872, for the transaction of congregational business, do instruct and authorize the trustees of said church to raise the sum of fifteen hundred dollars, and so comply with the conditions in said bequest."

On Apr. 14. 1873, the trustees took decisive action with reference to delinquents in pew rent; they resolved that the names of all delinquents in payment of their pew rent, with the several amounts, should be conspicuously posted in the vestibule of the church for the space of twenty days, and if said pew rent remained unpaid at the expiration of the above time, the accounts should be placed in legal hands for collection. At the same time the following rules were adopted for the government of the sexton :

FIRST. Ring the bell at the stated hours as given by the proper authority of the church.

SECOND. Sweep the body of the church, gallery &c., once each month; dust the seats every two weeks; basement to be kept clean, and all ashes, coal, cinders &c., to be kept from around the furnaces, and all unburnt coal to be screened—the church to furnish the screen.

THIRD. Lamps to be properly filled, trimmed and cleansed not less frequently than once in two weeks, or oftener if circumstances require it.

FOURTH. Fires to be built at the direction of the proper authorities as they at their discretion may deem necessary.

FIFTH. Gates to be properly opened and closed, and church grounds to be kept clear of all loose rubbish; the walks &c. to be kept clear of snow and other obstructions.

SIXTH. The grave-yard to be mowed twice each year, once in June and once in September, and not later in each month than the 15., the grass to be removed from the yard. The earth from the graves to be removed from each plot within one month from the time of digging of the grave, the dirt to be removed to any part of the yard designated by the trustees, the dirt removed to be properly leveled.

SEVENTH. The prices for digging graves shall not be less than three dollars nor exceed five dollars, the distinction to be made by the size of the grave. He shall open and prepare the church for all services held therein whether for funerals or other meetings.

The committee appointed to raise the $1500 reported Apr. 18. 1873, that they had "Eighteen hundred and fifty dollars on subscription, a portion of which remained uncollected." At this meeting the old board of trustees was reelected; Moses Robins and Wm. S. Gardner were elected to fill vacancies occasioned by the resignation of Joseph C. Smith and removal of Wm. S. Smith. At this meeting action was taken with reference to taking down the spire of the church and rebuilding the same, it having been struck by lightning. Wm. S. Gardner was appointed to have charge of these repairs. The trustees were duly authorized to employ a sexton at a salary not to exceed $100. At a meeting of the congregation held May 3. 1873, pursuant to adjournment on Apr. 18., the following action was taken relative to the spire of the church: "Resolved, that in view of the state of the steeple &c., that the trustees be authorized to proceed at once to repair it."

This year again we find evidence of disaffection in the congregation. On June 10. the session made the following minute: "The subject of the absence of many members of the church from the sacrament of the Lord's supper elicited careful consideration and a determination to examine into the causes and endeavor by God's guidance to overcome the evil." June 28. 1873, the trustees held a meeting, at which it was

"Resolved that the resolution in regard to posting delinquents, be carried out, and that the secretary be authorized to carry it into effect." At the same meeting it was "Resolved that the services of Hon. John T. Bird be secured to assist the church in securing the legacy of the late John P. Smith." "A notice from the solicitor of the estate of the late John P. Smith, notifying the board to appear in chancery at Trenton, N. J., on July 10, 1873, was then read, and on motion Daniel Williamson was authorized to borrow the will of the late John P. Smith from his widow for a short time for the use of the church in the matter of the legacy."

July 28, 1873, the trustees met. "On motion it was resolved to postpone notices of delinquents until the church should be ready for services." From this it would appear that the repairs consequent upon the church's being struck by lightning were now in progress. It was decided at this time to have the vestibule frescoed in oil instead of water colors as originally agreed upon. In connection with repairs upon the church there were some repairs made at the parsonage at this time. The ladies now raised money and refurnished the church and had the same neatly frescoed. At a meeting of the congregation held Aug. 14, 1873, the following action was taken with reference to repairs upon the church :

"*Resolved*, that the trustees of the First Presbyterian Church of Bloomsbury be instructed by said congregation to expend the balance of money on hand to finish painting said church in the inside, and on the outside if deemed necessary, and to carpet said church, together with any other repairs, if needed; and that the trustees shall give an order on the treasurer for the amount, who is authorized to pay the same out of the funds in his hands, that are not otherwise appropriated."

The damage to the church by lightning was assessed and paid by the insurance companies issuing the policies upon the building. It was out of these funds the above referred to expenses were to be paid. The trustees of the church felt that this was not a proper application of the funds in question and accordingly, in a meeting held Aug. 23, they

"*Resolved* that the board of trustees do hereby express their dissatisfaction with the action of the congregational meeting held on Aug. 14., in regard to the disposition of the moneys received from the insurance companies, said action being in opposition to the expressed wish of the whole board at a previous meeting, and it was further

Resolved, that a copy of this resolution be forwarded to the secretary of each insurance company." The contract for painting the church was then awarded, and Wm. S. Gardner, Theodore Tinsman and John S. Carter were appointed a committee on specifications, and to oversee the work.

CHAPTER V.

PASTORATE OF REV. MR. SCOTT CONTINUED. DIFFICULTIES.

Church to be used only for worship. Envelope system. Additional elder elected. Burial ground enlarged. Louise F. Kennedy Fund. Dissensions before Presbytery. Resignation of third pastor.

At a meeting of the session held Jan 31. 1874, there was an interchange of opinion on the subject of church finances and a determination manifested to "correct seeming irregularities of system." Also the repeatedly recurring "subject of absenteeism occupied the attention of session." The latter subject came up again in session Feb. 5., at which time three elders were appointed a committee to interview the church members who are habitually absent from church ordinances. At this same meeting the following action was taken, viz:

"*Whereas* this church edifice was dedicated unto the Great Head of the church, for the use of his worship, and

Whereas exhibitions and shows of a church desecrating character, injuriously affect the cause of religion and hinder spiritual growth, therefore

Resolved that this church shall be used for the Lord's worship and the maintenance of his ordinances, and any uses derogatory thereto will not be permitted."

The financial condition of the church at this time seems to have been satisfactory, as shown by the following action taken in congregational meeting, Apr. 11. 1874, viz:

"*Resolved* that a vote of thanks be tendered to Wm. J. Smith and Robert I. Smith for their efficient services in raising money, and their great financial ability in thus having raised sufficient funds to liquidate the indebtedness of the church."

At this meeting it was decided that the number of trustees should be three, and Moses Robins, Wm. Dalrymple and John Stute were elected to that office, It was also directed that the pew rents should be collected quarterly. Duplicates were to be made out one month previous to the time when the rents were due and two collectors were to receive the money, one for Warren and one for Hunterdon county. There being now only three trustees, they met Apr. 28. 1874, and assigned to each one his special duties. Moses Robins was to act as secretary and treasurer of the board; Wm Dalrymple was to attend to the furnishing of the church with coal, oil, lamps &c. John Stute was to see to needful repairs about the parsonage, employ sexton &c. Mr. Stute was elected president of the board, Nov. 28. of this year.

The question of collections for the boards of the church came up in session May 8. 1874, and the card and envelope system was adopted.

The question of absenteeism came up again in session May 26. 1874, at which time three members of session were appointed committees to visit certain delinquents with regard to their duties. These committees reported June 6. that the parties interviewed, except one, expressed willingness to return to duty. At this meeting however an elder was appointed to interview another delinquent. Report was made on delinquencies June 20., but with no definite result. June 27. session appointed another committee to visit certain other delinquents. The committee reported July 18., but no definite action was taken upon the report. The question of family visitation was considered by session on Sep. 20. but no definite action taken thereon. The same subject was up Sep. 24. and two elders were appointed to commence a family visitation the next week. All these things go to show that there was an unsettled state of affairs among the people which was causing anxiety among the members of session. Apr. 6. 1875, whilst certain cases of scandal had claimed the attention of session, citations were issued for the appearance of some of those who had been visited by committees, to answer for their absence from the ordinances.

Whilst the overseers of the spiritual affairs of the church are thus seen to be actively engaged in the duties devolving upon them, we find the secular officers were not idle. At a meeting of the trustees, Oct. 9. 1875, the following action was taken: "Resolved that we, as trustees, in the transaction of official business, adopt as the seal of the First Presbyterian Church of Bloomsbury, a red seal, commonly called a wafer, such as was used at the incorporation of said church." "It was further resolved that the president of the board of trustees (Mr. John Stute) be and hereby is authorized to execute a release and quit claim to Mrs. Sarah E. G. Smith, executrix of John P. Smith deceased, in the name and in the behalf of the First Presbyterian Church of Bloomsbury, New Jersey." The matter was duly attended to and the proper records made relative thereto, thus securing to the congregation Mr. Smith's legacy. At the same meeting of the trustees (Oct. 9. 1875), "It was further resolved that no one of the said board of trustees of the First Presbyterian Church of Bloomsbury contract any debts to the amount of five dollars and upward in behalf of said church without the consent of the whole board of trustees of said church." Feb. 14. 1876, "at a meeting of the trustees and elders of the First Presbyterian Church, held this day, it was resolved that the congregation adopt the card and envelope system for the coming year for the purpose of raising money to defray the incidental expenses of the church, and for missionary and sabbath-school purposes of said church." March 27. of this year (1876), the congregation held a meeting at which time the subject of electing additional elders was considered. It was decided to elect but one at this time. Accordingly the following persons were nominated, viz: Moses Robins, John S. Carter, John Hance, Wm. S. Hulsizer, Robert I. Smith, Theodore Tinsman and Joseph Willever. The vote being taken it was found Moses Robins was duly elected. The session met on Apr. 8. and arranged that the ordination of Mr. Robins as elder should take place on Sabbath 16. inst. following. The same day (Apr. 8. 1876.) there was a congregational meeting held, at which time Moses Robins, Valentine Young and John Stute were elected trustees. At this time also the $1000 legacy of John P. Smith was put at interest, and it was decided that "The interest only of said legacy of one thousand dollars be used by said church without the consent of two thirds of said congregation at a regularly called meeting of said congregation." The same day in congregational meeting assembled, it was "Resolved that the pews of those who shall neglect to pay the assessment on the same within ten days after it shall become due, shall be declared vacant." As was customary, the trustees elected at this meeting, organized by electing John Stute president; and Moses Robins secretary and treasurer. Mr. Stute was appointed to look after repairs about the parsonage, employ sexton &c.; and Mr. Young was to attend to the procuring of coal, oil, lamps &c. In minutes of session Apr. 17. 1876, we find further evidence of the disturbed internal condition of the church. Complaint had been made to session with reference to alleged "unchristian action of two members of this church." an elder was appointed to notify the complainant that the session was ready to take up the case. Thereupon "the clerk was ordered to transmit a letter of citation to said [complainant] requiring him to appear before session on the 27. of April, at 2 o'clock, P. M., to confirm the charges or give reasons why they should be withdrawn." In connection with the same matter the session received, on Apr. 27., "a letter from [complainant] which was deemed inadmissible because of its being informal, and the subject matter was continued and the clerk was ordered to transmit a letter of citation to [complainant] requiring him to appear before session regarding certain charges by him made against certain two members of this church, at a meeting to be held on Saturday, the sixteenth of May ensuing, in the church, at 2 o'clock P. M."

At this same meeting (Apr. 27. 1876) a member of the church asked for a letter of dismission to unite with the Greenwich Presbyterian church. The cause of this was recognized to be the disturbed state of affairs in the church. Accordingly an elder was appointed a committee to advise with the applicant with reference to the matter. This however was of no avail and the member took his certificate, Mar. 6., and joined the neighboring church, together with three others who left for the same reasons that actuated him.

At the meeting of May 6., the complainant above referred to "appeared before session and asked leave to withdraw certain avowed intention of making charges against certain two members of this church." The request was granted and so the matter ended. The elders who had been appointed to make family visitations, reported May 13. 1876, "that they received much cordiality from the people and invitations to renew their visits." At this time (May 13. 1876) two more members were dismissed to join the neighboring church of Greenwich, the cause being the unsettled condition of the church.

Apr. 7. 1877, the people assembled in congregational meeting and elected Wm. Tinsman, Valentine Young and Moses Robins trustees. Mr. Young declined to serve and John Hance was elected in his place. The same day the trustees held a meeting, at which Wm. Tinsman was elected president; John Hance secretary; and Moses Robins treasurer.

Aug. 30. the internal commotions of the church again come to the surface in sessional meeting. The committee appointed to wait upon certain absentees was continued with instructions to report at the meeting to be held on Saturday, the 8. of September ensuing."

The congregation held a meeting Dec. 8. 1877, for the purpose of en-

larging the burial ground. At this time the following action was taken, viz:

Resolved 1. That the two lots, fifty feet each, making one hundred
feet by one hundred and fifty feet, and lying contiguous to the grave-
yard, and purchased for burial purposes, be enclosed on three sides
with a good substantial fence, and the said grounds put in proper condition for burial purposes.

Resolved 2. That the money received from said lands or plots be set
apart and not used for other purposes.

Resolved 3. That the price for lots sold be the same as the old plots,
and sold only for cash or on good and approved security.

Dec. 31. 1877, the dissensions in the congregation are again noticed
by session. The committee in one case of absenteeism "reported favorably." At the same time two elders were appointed a committee to
wait upon certain other parties relative to their delinquencies. A
committee was also appointed to wait upon a member of session "in relation to his absence from the stated means of grace." The member of
session being present, explained that "physical disability in his family
and in his own case caused his absence from church during the past
four Sabbaths." A second committee was appointed at this time to
wait upon another derelict church member. Jan. 19. 1878, "The committee to visit certain parties reported in part, and the same was accepted and the committee continued in one of the cases under consideration. At this meeting of Jan. 19. 1878, a communication relative to the
sabbath-school was considered but action thereon deferred. The matter
however came up again Feb. 4., at which time it was decided to appoint
officers in the school for one year. Elder Wm. J. Smith was appointed superintendent, Robert I. Smith treasurer, Peter Hulsizer librarian,
and elder Robins secretary. The session, as a committee, undertook
the procuring of a library. The envelope system of collections for benevolent objects and incidental expenses, which had been in use for
some time, was at this meeting (Feb. 4. 1878) ordered discontinued

until the end of May ensuing, and a semi-monthly collection was taken in its place. At this time the Louise F. Kennedy Fund, for the benefit of the poor of the congregation was established. The young lady whose name the fund bears was a daughter of elder Henry R. Kennedy. Dying in the bloom of womanhood she did not fail to remember the church of which she was a member and that in behalf of the Lord's unfortunate ones. In accordance with her wishes her father, after her death, carried out her scheme by making over to the congregation three shares of the capital stock of the Bloomsbury National Bank for this purpose.

Apr. 21. 1878, at a congregational meeting, Wm. S. Hulsizer was elected trustee to fill the place of Dr. Creveling who declined to serve. On the 27. the trustees organized by electing Wm. S. Hulsizer, president; John Hance, secretary; and Moses Robins, treasurer.

The dissensions which, as we have seen, existed in the congregation, came before Presbytery in the spring of 1878. We find the following in the minutes of Presbytery, Apr. 10, 1878, relative to the matter, viz:

"Papers purporting to come from the congregation of Bloomsbury having been placed in the hands of the Moderator, they are ordered to be referred to a special committee." "The Moderator announced as this committee, Rev. A. A. Haines, Rev. J. M. Maxwell and ruling elder J. G. Shipman." This committee reported as follows, viz: "The committee report that in the minutes of the congregational meeting furnished them, no Commissioner was appointed to this Presbytery, and the whole difficulty seems to arise from the disaffection of a very few persons with the pastor; and that the committee cannot find that there is any difficulty existing in the church to render it necessary for Presbytery to send a committee to them. They therefore recommend that the request to send a committee to the church of Bloomsbury, and the papers be returned to the person handing them in." This action on the part of Presbytery did not have the effect of healing matters contrariwise seemed to put fuel upon the fire. One evidence of this was manifested in the immediate expression of a desire on the part of members of the church to be dismissed to other churches. May 11. 1878.

seven persons asked for letters of dismission, two of whom, it was alleged desired to join the neighboring church of Greenwich. In the case of these two objection was made to granting the request on the ground that it was believed by members of session that the parties had changed their minds, and had made no written application for dismission. As the time for the fall meeting of Presbytery drew near the different factions manifested renewed activity. In the minutes of session, Sep. 7, 1878, it was recorded that an elder started the subject of electing a delegate to the next meeting of Presbytery, whereupon the moderator spoke adversely thereto and left the room. In the minutes of Presbytery, Oct. 1, 1878, we read: "Certain papers having been placed in the hands of the Moderator for the consideration of the Presbytery they were ordered to be referred to a committee." This committee consisted of Revs. J. J. Crane, J. P. Clarke and ruling elder Mr. John White. This committee reported recommending that the papers in question be placed in the hands of the Judicial Committee. The Judicial Committee's report in the matter is as follows: "The second paper placed in the hands of the committee, referring to matters connected with the congregation at Bloomsbury, is one of which the committee is divided in judgment. But it being reported that serious difficulties exist in that congregation the committee recommend that a committee of three ministers and two elders be appointed to visit it during the month of December next, to inquire into its state, and to report at such meeting of the Presbytery as the Moderator shall call in pursuance of its request." "The following were appointed the committee called for in the above report: Rev. A. A. Haines, Rev. Alexander Proudfit, Rev. J. F. Shaw, and ruling elders Thomas Ryerson, M. D. and Mr. Charles E. Vail." "The committe, to which was referred a paper which had been placed in the hands of the Moderator for the cosideration of the Presbytery, made a report, that it found said paper purporting to be a petition from certain members of the church of Bloomsbury, with reference to three ruling elders of that church: that it found the paper to be in order and laid it before Presbytery for such action as it deemed proper. The report was accepted and the paper was ordered to be re-

ferred to the committee appointed to visit the congregation at Bloomsbury." In the minutes of the Presbytery, Dec. 17., at Oxford First
Church, the following records were made relative to or bearing upon
these difficulties:

"Two ruling elders of the church of Bloomsbury,   *   *   appearing in the Presbytery as the representatives of the session of said
church, the question as to the representative claims of these elders was
referred to a committee, consisting of Rev. H. E. Spayd, Rev. J. B.
Kugler, and ruling elder J. G. Shipman." This committee reported as
follows: "The Committee appointed to decide who is the legally appointed delegate from the church of Bloomsbury to this Presbytery, report that they have examined the minutes of the session and they find
that on Sep. 36. 1878, at a meeting of the session of the church, elder *
*   * was appointed a delegate to the meeting of Presbytery, which
was to meet at Greenwich, on the first of October, then next ensuing
and for no other meeting of Presbytery. There is no authentic minute
of any delegate having been appointed to this meeting of the Presbytery, and the committee therefore report that in their judgment, according to the second decision of the Assembly, the session of the Bloomsbury church has no elder legally appointed to this Presbytery."

The report of the committee to visit the church is as follows: "The
committee appointed by Presbytery to visit the church of Bloomsbury
during the month of December, to inquire into its state, would report
that they visited the church on the 3. inst.   A full hearing was afforded to all who presented themselves on that and the following day.
The following paper was subsequently placed in the hands of the committee.   Rev. H. B. Scott offers his resignation of the pastorate of the
First Presbyterian Church of Bloomsbury, said resignation to take
effect on the first day of January, 1879, and he promises to remove
from the town of Bloomsbury by the first day of March, 1879, and the
representatives of the church promising that they will pay Mr. Scott
all arrears of salary by January 1. 1879, and six months salary in addition, three hundred dollars on April 1. 1879, and three hundred dollars
on July 1. 1879. [Signed.]   H. B. Scott, Moses Robins, Jos. C. Smith,

(trustee), Wm. Tinsman, H. R. Kennedy, Wm. J. Smith, Wm. Dalrymple. Robert I. Smith, John Gardner. Theo. Tinsman.   The committee would recommend that the resignation of Rev H. B. Scott be accepted. to take effect Jan. 1. 1879, and that the church be required to pay the money promised in the above agreement.   Rev. Mr. Scott then presented his resignation as pastor of the congregation at Bloomsbury. The representatives from said congregation, and who having signed the above paper, appeared in the Presbytery and signified their acquiescence to the resignation of their pastor, when it was

Resolved, That the Rev. H. B. Scott having presented his resignation as pastor of the First Presbyterian Church of Bloomsbury, to take effect on the first day of January, 1879, it be accepted, and that the pastoral relation be dissolved, the dissolution to take effect at the time mentioned." "Rev. Wm. Thomson was appointed to preach in the church at Bloomsbury on Jan. 5. 1879, and declare the pulpit vacant. Mr. Thomson was likewise appointed moderator of the session of the church of Bloomsbury during and for the time the said church is without a pastor."

In accordance with this appointment Mr. Thomson preached in the church on Jan. 5. 1879, and declared the pulpit vacant.   Thus ended the pastorate of Rev. H. B. Scott.   During the nine years and a half of his ministrations there were received into church by profession of their faith in Christ one hundred and six persons, and forty-one by certificate.

CHAPTER VI.

PASTORATE OF REV. MR. CLYDE.

Unsettled difficulties.   Low spiritual state.   Benevolent work suffering.   Diffi-

culties carried before Synod. Election of fourth pastor. Presbyterian Hymnal adopted. Attempt to organize a new church. Audience room relighted. Discipline. Debt of church paid. Lecture-room refitted. End of difficulties in the church. Death of elder William Tinsman. Improved condition of congregation. New side-walks.

It would seem that the Presbytery, at its meeting in December, 1878, congratulated itself that all the difficulties in the Bloomsbury church had been settled. In this however, they were sadly deceived. Jan. 5, 1879, the very day the pulpit was declared vacant, there was a meeting of session held, moderated by Rev. Wm. Thomson, at which the librarian of the sabbath-school sent in his resignation, said resignation growing out of the troubles in the church, as it was understood. It was proposed at this meeting also to appoint a committee to wait on ten members of the church with reference to their derelictions in duty. The design however, we believe was not carried into effect.

Mar. 23, (or Apr. 5,) 1879, the congregation elected Robert I. Smith, Jesse J. Lake and John Hance, trustees.

The difficulties in the church, which we have seen were not settled, it would seem assumed two leading characteristics, viz: some in the congregation desired the removal of the pastor, others the removal of a part of the session. To meet the exigencies of the case with reference to both parties, Presbytery had secured the resignation of the pastor, and directly or indirectly advised the congregation to elect additional elders if they were not satisfied with those in office. Accordingly Mar. 31, 1879, the following action was taken, viz:

Resolved, The session have long been impressed that the spiritual wants of the people living in the upper or eastern section of the church territory, demand that a ruling elder be located in their midst, so as to enable more efficient and prompt spiritual care, therefore

Resolved, That the session of this church accord opportunity for the election of one or more ruling elders whenever the members of the church or a majority thereof express such desire or the Presbytery shall take order thereto.

In the report to Presbytery adopted at this meeting (Mar. 31, 1879)

the following appears, viz: "The attendance of communicants on sacramental occasions has not been so large as in former years, and the congregation of worshipers has diminished." "By order of Presbytery the Rev. Wm. Thomson preached on the fifth of January and declared the pulpit vacant. Ministerial supplies (appointed by the committee) have preached regularly since that period, and there is a marked increase in the number and better attention on the part of the worshipers. Quiet prevails, and the word is received with manifest edification." "Contributions for the boards of the church have been almost entirely neglected." "In order to obtain a better knowledge of the spiritual wants of the people they propose to make a series of family visitations as soon as practicable."

The administration of affairs by the session however, was not acceptable to that portion of the congregation which desired the removal of certain elders. The Presbytery therefore, at its stated meeting, Apr. 9. 1879, found itself confronted with the old difficulties, as will be seen from the following record:

"The committee to which was referred a certain paper placed in the hands of the moderator for the consideration of Presbytery, presented the following report: The committee appointed to examine and report upon a paper put into the hands of the moderator finds said paper to be a petition purporting to come from a majority of the communicants of the church of Bloomsbury, in accordance with the advice of Presbytery given at the meeting at the First Presbyterian Church of Oxford, Dec. 18. 1878, praying Presbytery to advise the session of that church to take order for the retirement of certain elders from service in that church, or to take such action as the Presbytery may deem best to secure their removal. The committee recognizes the right of petition in general. It cannot admit however, that it is correct to say that Presbytery has given advice that that right be exercised in this case. On the contrary we believe that the action taken at Oxford was, and was intended to be a definitive settlement of the matters then in dispute. This was the intent of the agreement which stands on the records of Presbytery signed by those who were regarded as representatives of all interests involved This being so, we cannot but regard the presentation of the petition as an infringement upon that agreement: and for the Presbytery to act in a favorable sense upon this petition would be to make itself a party to a breach of faith. We recommend therefore that the petition be returned to those from whom it purports to come." This report was adopted, whereupon "Rev. H. B. Scott, in behalf of the petitioners whose names are attached to the above paper, gave notice of his intention to appeal and complain to the Synod of New Jersey against this action of the Presbytery."

At this meeting of Presbytery, the session was granted permission to supply their own pulpit till the next stated meeting of Presbytery. Accordingly we find the following action taken Apr. 26.:

Whereas, Presbytery consented to supply the pulpit of this church until the next stated meeting, but it is now thought best to secure a pastor so soon as the congregation shall be satisfied, therefore

Resolved, That with the consent of the committee of conference we now proceed to hear candidates for the pastorate."

After hearing a limited number of candidates the following action was taken May 25. 1879:

Whereas, The session of this church having had a number of applications from the membership of this church to elect a pastor from the candidates heard, being satisfied that it is for the best interests of the church that the election be proceeded with as soon as convenient, therefore

Resolved, That Thursday, June 5., this congregation will proceed to the above request.

Through the difficulties in the church the people found themselves involved in indebtedness, and accordingly a meeting of the congregation was held, Apr. 17. 1879. The meeting convened in pursuance of the following notice, viz: "Apr. 6. 1879. There will be a meeting of the congregation of the First Presbyterian Church of Bloomsbury, N. J. in the basement of the church, on Thursday, the 17. day of April instant, at two o'clock P. M., to take into consideration the financial condition of the church, and to make disposition of money placed in their hands: said trustees owing to present circumstances desire instructions from the congregation." The trustees account book was examined and the indebtedness of the church ascertained, whereupon the following action was taken:

Whereas, By the last will and testament of John P. Smith, dec'd, the sum of one thousand dollars was bequeathed to the First Presbyterian Church of Bloomsbury, of which sum the interest only could be used the principal to remain in tact, unless by a two thirds vote of said congregation said principal to be used if needed, therefore

Resolved 1st. That the urgent needs of this church require the use of this money to liquidate the present indebtedness of this church.

Resolved 2d, That this meeting held this 17. day of Apr. 1879, called by the trustees of said church, do hereby decide by a vote of the congregation to authorize said trustees to use this money for the above named purpose, namely, the cancelling said indebtedness of this church."

At a congregational meeting held on June 5, 1879, the people proceeded to the election of a pastor. The following were placed in nomination, viz: Rev. John C. Clyde, Rev. H. B. Townsend and Rev. E. A. Hamilton. The election resulted in the choice of Rev. John C. Clyde.

The call was made out at a salary of eight hundred dollars a year, payable quarterly, with free use of the parsonage, and a vacation of four Sabbaths annually. A proposition was made that the electors sign the call, which failed. It was then proposed that three of the oldest members sign it, which was also lost. Finally it was ordered that the session and trustees should sign it. This reveals the distrust which existed among the people as to the future welfare of the church.

Rev. Mr. Clyde in due time expressed his willingness to accept the call, and commenced his labors among the people July 1. 1879. The work from the outset was a delicate, difficult and discouraging one. The church was distracted through the long continued and fierce dissensions which had existed in its midst. The people were therefore in no condition to go forward in the work of building up the church either spiritually or temporally. The whole community was affected by the turmoil in the church. There were many hard words spoken and harder thoughts entertained by those who were professedly the followers of the meek and lowly Jesus. Many seemed to assume that the newly elected pastor was their enemy and it devolved upon them to treat him disrespectfully and unkindly. Taken all in all the field was in about as uninviting a condition as it well could be. Notwithstanding this it had to be assumed that here as elsewhere, the gospel was to be preached: the authority of the church sustained: and God's true children harmonized and fed if possible, and to the accomplishment of this task the pastor addressed himself. One line of policy adopted was to draw the minds of the people away from the troubles and interest them, if possible, in church work. It was thought the adoption of a new book of praise would be a benefit to the church. Accordingly in July 1879, a congregational meeting was held with reference to the adoption of a new book. The session, trustees and choir were to constitute a committee to recommend some suitable collection. The committee met Aug. 10, 1879, at which time the Presbyterian Hymnal was adopted.

July 20, 1879, Rev. John C. Clyde, pastor elect, first moderated the session. At a meeting of session, Sep. 13, 1879, "action was taken with reference to the installation of Rev. John C. Clyde, and the delegate to Presbytery was instructed to ask the same to appoint Rev Wm. Thomson to preside, preach the sermon and propose the constitutional questions: Rev. Thomas S. Long to charge the pastor; and Rev. H. B. Townsend to charge the people. The delegate was also instructed to ask Presbytery to appoint Tuesday, Oct. 14. at 2 o'clock P. M., as the time at which the installation should take place."

At a meeting of Presbytery at Asbury, Oct 7. 1879, the pastor elect "presented a letter of dismission and recommendation from the Presbytery of Chester, with a request that he be received as a member of this Presbytery. The certificate having been read was found to be in order, and Rev. Mr. Clyde was received according to his request, and his name ordered to be placed upon the roll."

The call having been presented to and accepted by the pastor elect, Oct. 14., at 2 o'clock P. M., was fixed as the time of installation. Rev. Wm. Thomson was appointed to preside, propose the constitutional questions and charge the pastor: Rev. John B. Kugler to preach the sermon: and Rev. H. B. Townsend to charge the people. The installation services were duly held at the time appointed. At this same meeting of Presbytery, while efforts were being made to advance the interests of the church, there were some who were exerting themselves to cripple it. As we have seen, notice had been given on the part of some of the congregation, of an intention to appeal from a decision of the Presbytery relative to the difficulties in the church. So at this meeting "a paper was placed in the hands of the moderator which was read and found to be a complaint from a part of the church of Bloomsbury, with the reasons therefor, to the Synod of New Jersey, against the action of the Presbytery at its meeting in April last, whereupon Rev. A. A. Haines and Rev. W. A. Holliday were appointed counsel to defend the action of Presbytery before Synod." The case came up in Synod at its meeting in Trenton, on Oct. 22, 1879, and was tried in the usual form. Rev. Dr. Kempshall and Rev. David Stevenson acting as counsel for the complainants by appointment of Synod. The final vote was taken with the following result, viz: "To confirm the action of Presbytery 48; to confirm in part 4; to reverse the action of Presbytery 41; to reverse in part 6." The moderator declared that the vote was to confirm the action of Presbytery. Dr. Craven announced his dissent from that decision. Dr. Duffield, Dr. Craven and elder Baker were appointed a committee to bring in a minute setting forth the reasons for the decision rendered." This committee brought in a majority and minority report, the former of which was adopted and was as follows, viz:

"The vote of the Synod being forty-eight to confirm, four to confirm in part; forty-one to reverse, six to reverse in part the decision of the Presbytery complained against, it is the judgment of the Synod that the decision of the Presbytery be confirmed. That, in view of the nearly equally divided vote, and the expression of the opinions of members of Synod preceding the vote, it is recommended to the Presbytery of Newton that should a memorial be presented from a majority of the Bloomsbury church, asking a change in the eldership, it should receive respectful and deliberate consideration. Also, that in future they keep a more careful and particular record of their proceedings. The Synod would also at the same time recommend to the members of the church at Bloomsbury to seek the things that make for peace."

This disposition of the case, it would seem, ought to have been satisfactory to all parties interested, but such was not the case. In due time notice was given to the moderator of Synod of the intention of certain persons to appeal to the General Assembly from the decision of the Synod. The moderator of Synod wrote to the pastor of the church with a view of arriving at such solution of the difficulties as would stop litigation. The pastor gave such advice and information as in his judgment, would be calculated to bring about a better understanding between the litigants. Fortunately through this or some other means the case was prevented from going before the General Assembly, but affairs remained in an unsettled condition until the absence of any complaint before the Assembly in the spring of 1880 confirmed the action of Synod in its settlement of the difficulties.

Whilst many of those who upheld the appeal and complaint to Synod against Presbytery accepted Synod's action as final and continued to perform their christian duties in the church, others manifested an unwillingness to submit to the authority of the church, and made an effort to carry on religious services in a public hall in the village without consulting Presbytery and without taking certificates of dismission from the church to which they belonged. This effort at continued resistance to the regularly constituted authorities of the church however, failed after a few weeks.

Notwithstanding there were these great obstacles in the way of progress, the policy of going straight forward with the affairs of the church was persevered in. As we have seen Presbytery advised the adoption of means whereby the grounds of complaint with reference to certain elders might be removed, and this was also recommended by the Synod. Accordingly the following action was taken Nov. 13, 1879:

"The session having considered on the 31. of March last the propriety of giving the congregation an opportunity of expressing their views on the subject of electing additional elders, took up the same subject at this meeting. After consideration it was

Resolved 1st. That the moderator be instructed to give notice on next Sabbath morning, Nov. 16., that the congregation would be convened in congregational meeting on Sabbath morning Nov. 23., after service to give expression to their views on the above subject.

Resolved 2d. That if the congregation see fit to elect additional elders they shall be afforded then and there an opportunity to proceed to said election if so disposed.

The meeting of the congregation here contemplated was duly held Nov. 23. 1879, at the close of divine service. The pastor was elected chairman of the meeting and Wm. S. Creveling, M. D., secretary. The call as formulated at the meeting of session Nov. 13. was read. "A motion was made and seconded that additional elders be elected. After a full and free discussion of the subject, the motion was lost. The congregation having decided not to elect elders, and no further business being before the meeting. on motion it adjourned."

At a meeting of session Jan. 16. 1880, "The officers of the congregational meeting referred to in the minutes of the meeting of session, were requested to record their minutes in the session book for permanent preservation and convenience of access and reference." This request was acceded to and the minutes of the meeting so recorded.

In order that the people might have their attention occupied with the interests of the church, at the holidays in 1879, a public dinner and oyster supper were held in the public hall of the village, at which time a handsome sum was realized for miscellaneous expenses. and this has been an annual feature of church work at this season of the year since that time.

With the opening of the year 1880, a mite society was started which accumulated funds also for miscellaneous needs.

In order to make the main audience-room of the church more cheerful, new lighting arrangements were secured and placed therein.

The annual congregational meeting was held Apr. 3. 1880, at which time Jesse J. Lake. John Hance and Robert I. Smith were elected trustees. The same day the board elected Jesse J. Lake, president; John Hance, secretary; and R. I. Smith, treasurer. It becoming manifested (by the absence of an appeal to the General Assembly in 1880, on the part of those who were not satisfied with the decision of Synod in 1879) that the litigation growing out of the troubles in the church had ceased, attention was turned to the correction of evils which were found to exist in the church. One of these evils was the old one of neglect of the ordinances: another was the retention upon the roll of the names of those who had removed beyond the bounds of the congregation or attended other churches, and who either neglected or refused to take certificates of dismission, whilst at the same time they were to a greater or less extent taking part in the control of the affairs of the church. To correct these evils, on Sep. 11, 1880, session selected such decisions of the General Assembly as bore upon these points, and directed the clerk to forward a copy of the same to the membership of the church for their guidance. At this meeting elder Smith resigned his position as superintendent of the sabbath-school, which was accepted upon condition of his continuance until a suitable person could be found to take his place.

In the report to Presbytery adopted by session Apr. 2, 1881, the following is found, viz: "The spiritual condition of the church seems to have improved somewhat, whilst much is yet to be hoped for in this particular. Efforts have been made during the year to ascertain the real numerical strength of the congregation. A small debt upon the church has been paid during the year. A mite society has been successfully carried on; and having relighted the main audience room, the congregation proceeded to raise funds for the benefit of the sabbath-school. The accommodations of the school in the lecture room have been greatly improved. The unsightly wooden supports which made the room so unattractive, have been replaced by suitable iron ones: the uncomfortable wooden benches have been replaced by chairs: the pulpit has been altered and the room generally renovated and relighted. A new sabbath-school library has been purchased and hymn books provided whereby the children sing the same hymns that are used in the regular church service. During the year the invested charitable funds of the congregation have been made available and used for the purpose for which they were provided."

The action of Sep. 11, 1880, having been communicated to the congregation, and some of the delinquents not seeming to heed the admonition then given, the following action was taken by session Apr. 2. 1881, viz:

Whereas, General Assembly (Digest page 624, 9.) has enjoined upon sessions of our churches, on the removal of any members beyond boundaries of their own organization, to furnish such members, whether in full communion or members by baptism only, with testimonials of their standing, which testimonials it shall be the duty of such persons at once to present to some church of our connection, and the session shall earnestly counsel these members to transfer their relation immediately if practicable, or at the earliest opportunity, therefore it was

Resolved, That the clerk of session be and hereby is ordered to forward testimonials of regular standing at the time of their removal, in accordance with this action, to the following absent members, viz: * * By this means the roll was to some extent revised.

Apr. 1881, the congregation elected Jesse J. Lake, John Hance and Robert I. Smith, trustees. The same day the trustees elected Jesse J. Lake, president; John Hance, secretary; and Robert I. Smith, treasurer.

Having on April 2, dealt with the delinquents who resided beyond the bounds of the congregation, session proceeded to consider the case of those who resided within bounds. Accordingly May 28, 1881, "Session convened in accordance with Chap. IX, sec. 7. Form of Gov't, at the request of two elders." "The subject of the absence from the ordinances of the church on the part of certain members was taken up and action of Assembly (Digest Book II, Ch. I. 12, a.) bearing upon the points, was read. It was decided to proceed in the present case under this provision. The following charge, upon common fame, was formulated, viz: Unchristian conduct; specification, wilful absenting from the ordinances of the church." Under this charge twenty-three persons were held. After fixing June 2. as the time of next meeting and entering the names of the witnesses who were to prove the charge, the clerk was directed to cite the parties to appear at that time, and an el der was appointed to conduct the prosecution. It was decided to sit in private, in accordance with act of Assembly, 1880, minutes page 23.

June 2. 1881, session convened pursuant to adjournment, at 9.30 o' clock A. M. The elder who was appointed to have charge of the prose cution not being present another was appointed in his place. Before proceeding to judicial session, for reasons satisfactory to session, the charge was withdrawn with reference to three of the persons held, leaving twenty persons under process. Having proceeded to judicial session the names of the accused were called for the purpose of pre senting them with a copy of the charge and names of the witnesses. One only appeared who pleaded guilty, expressed penitence and was admonished. The clerk was directed to issue citations for the witness es, and those who had failed to appear at this meeting, to appear at a meeting to be held June 14., for trial. Session accordingly convened June 14. 1881, at 8 o'clock A. M. Upon calling the names of the accus ed only one appeared. The charge having been presented he pleaded guilty and retired whilst session considered what action should be ta ken in the case. When recalled he failed to appear and was accord ingly suspended from the communion of the church, in accordance with act of Assembly, Digest page 493, a. The remaining eighteen accused persons not appearing, "the clerk was ordered to cite these, with the witnesses, to appear at the next meeting for trial," whereupon session adjourned to meet June 18. 1881. The names of the eighteen remain ing accused persons were called, none of whom appeared; thus sus pending themselves from the communion of the church without the ac tion of session, by operation of the law of the church provided in such cases. "Session thereupon declared that these persons were excluded from the communion of the church for their contumacy until they re pent, in accordance with Book of Discipline, Chap. 4. sec 40."

An elder was appointed to have charge of the cases and session pro ceeded to place on record the proof of the charge preferred. "In accordance with Book of Discipline Chap. 4, sec. 19, it was deemed expedient not to publish the action of session beyond the judicatory."

Under date of June 27, 1881, six of the persons who had been suspended from the communion of the church gave notice of their intention to appeal and complain to Presbytery, but never carried the matter further. Thus for the time being, at least, ended the troubles in the church.

At this time the congregation was called upon to undergo a sad bereavement. Elder William Tinsman, who had served the church from its organization, and who was a zealous participant in taking the initiatory steps in the cases of discipline which he, with the other members of session felt were needed for the welfare of the church, was stricken of apoplexy and died June 4.

The following report of session to Presbytery was made Mar. 25, 1882.

The ordinances have been maintained uninterruptedly throughout the year, and the fruits thereof exhibited in the reception of a number of new converts into the membership of the church, and the manifestly increased earnestness in the hearing of the preached word by the entire congregation. The revision of the roll and the consequently corrected table of figures elucidates more clearly the actual strength of the church, and although the number of communicants reported is less than it was in last year's report, the moral and spiritual power of the church is much stronger. The fact that the congregation has been steadily increasing through the adherence of persons moving into the community, and through the increased interest of some residing in the village, the church is financially stronger. There has been a marked improvement in the attendance, perhaps more especially prominent since the series of services during the Presbyterial visitation. The interest apparent on that occasion has not subsided and we have manifest evidence that the Holy Spirit is in our midst. The standard of piety is higher among the members of the church. The attachment to the pastor and to each other is a prominent feature, and all things considered the church has much reason for thankfulness."

Apr. 8, 1882, the congregation elected Charles Alpaugh, J. J. Lake and L. Anderson, trustees. At this meeting it was ordered that "no burial plots be sold to any persons outside of this congregation." Apr. 9. Robert I. Smith and John Hance were elected trustees to take the places of J. J. Lake and L. Anderson who declined to serve. The same day the trustees elected Charles Alpaugh, president: John Hance, secretary; and R. I. Smith, treasurer.

The sidewalks leading to the church becoming dilapidated, the congregation united with the Methodist Episcopal church of the village in an excursion to New York and Coney Island to repair the same for the mutual benefit of the two congregations. The excursion came off Aug. 11, 1882, and was a gratifying success. The annual holiday supper was given on Christmas, and the funds realized therefrom set apart to complete the sum needed for sidewalks, and for the use of the sabbath-school. In pursuance of the original intention, stone flagging was laid down in front of all the church property contiguous to the public streets of the village, except on the south side, where it was deemed not necessary.

In the spring of 1883, the following report of the condition of the church was made to Presbytery, viz:

1. The preaching of the word and the ordinances of the church have been regularly maintained throughout the past year. 2. The number of worshipers has perceptibly increased, and their earnest attention and deep interest are quite apparent. 3. The admission of a number of new converts into the communion and christian fellowship of the church, confirms the belief that the Spirit is in our midst, and strengthens the hope that God will yet bless his means toward an abundant conversion of souls. 4. Notwithstanding there have been removals by death and dismissals to other churches, the reception of members upon confession of Christ and by letter, render an increased total of communicants. 5. The moral and spiritual power of the church is steadily growing stronger. Than in the past brotherly love and christian charity have become a marked feature. Perhaps during the entire history of the church there has never been such close accord with the people and their pastor. 6. The congregation is growing numerically stronger

because of adherence of families moving into the village, and the more cordial support of earlier residents. 7. Although not possessed of such ample means as in former years, the church is growing in financial strength. There is no indebtedness; but on the contrary there is a considerable fund set apart for incidental purposes; besides a fund for the relief of the poor of the church. All things considered, the session are encouraged to hope for a bright future for the church.

Such was substantially the condition of the church July 1. 1883, the close of the first four years of the pastorate of Rev. John C. Clyde. Up to this time there had been received into the church thirty-four persons, fifteen upon profession of their faith in Christ; and nineteen by certificate. Nineteen infants had been baptized, and eight couples married.

——— 0 ———

SUBSCRIBERS
FOR THE
HISTORY OF THE FIRST PRESBYTERIAN CHURCH OF
BLOOMSBURY, NEW JERSEY.

Names.	Copies.
Henry R. Kennedy	4.
William J. Smith	2.
Moses Robins	2.
Robert I. Smith	3.
John C. Smith	2.
Louis Anderson	1.
William S. Creveling, M. D.	1.
David Wean	1.
Franklin P. Cline	1.
James J. Willever	1.
S. R. Dalrymple	1.
A. W. Creveling	1.
Thomas S. Hoffman	1.
John Hance	1.
William C. Smith	1.
Theodore Melick	1.
William Fulmer	1.
M. J. Vliet	1.
Elizabeth Smith	1.
J. G. Apgar	1.
Wm. Carling	1.

64   *First Presbyterian Church of Bloomsbury.*

Theodore Tinsman	1.
A. C. Smith, M. D.	1.
Charles Alpaugh	1.
Joseph Stopp	1.
C. H. Smith	1.
S. E. G. Smith	1.
W. G. Smith	1.
Wm. Little, M. D.	1.
A. G. Creveling	1.
Henry M. Vliet	1.
George Vliet	1.
Eliza Vliet	1.
Alice V. Vliet	1.
Rachel Tinsman	1.
Lizzie Emery	1.
James H. Willever	2.
Hannah A. Creveling	1.
Agnes Creveling	1.
Charles O. Creveling	1.
James L. Creveling	1.
C. M. Williamson	1.
Mr. Brotzman	1.
J. W. DeHart	1.
V. R. Wolverton	1.
Mary V. Smith	1.
Sarah C. Smith	1.
Ellie Smith	1.
Mary P. Young	1.
Wm. Dalrymple	1.
P. L. Hawk	1.
George Hawk	1.
Mr. Bulmer	1.
James Myers	1.

John Sidders	1.
Samuel Hanson	1.
J. C. Stewart, M. D.	1.
A. Creveling	1.
G. Cole	1.
Wm. Sherrer	1.
George Creamer	1.
John W. Creveling	1.
S. N. Park	1.
John Wieder	1.
George Carpenter	1.
George Streepy	1.
John L. Allen	1.
George Opdyke	1-
S. Probasco	1.
Henry Gardner	1.
Isaac Wolverton	1.
George Race	1.
Lewis Fox	1.

—— 0 ——

Other Publications by Rev. John C. Clyde.

History of the Allen Township Presbyterian Church and the Community which has sustained it, in what was formerly known as the Irish Settlement, Northampton County, Pa.   1876, pp. 200.   75c.

Genealogies, Necrology and Reminiscences of the Irish Settlement, or a Record of those Scotch-Irish Presbyterian families who were the First Settlers in the "Forks of Delaware," now Northampton County, Pennsylvania—a Sequel to the "History of the Allen Township Presbyterian Church.   1879, pp. 420. $1.00.

Rosbrugh, a Tale of the Revolution, or Life, Labors and Death of Rev. John Rosbrugh, pastor of Greenwich, Oxford and Mansfield Woodhouse (Washington) Presbyterian churches, N. J., from 1764 to 1769; and of Allen Township church, Pa., from 1769 to 1777; Chaplain in the Continental Army; Clerical Martyr of the Revolution, killed by Hessians, in the battle of Assunpink, at Trenton, New Jersey, Jan. 2d, 1777.   Founded upon a paper read before the New Jersey Historical Society at its meeting in Trenton, Jan. 15th, 1880; to which is appended genealogical data of all the Rosbrughs of the connection in America.   1880, pp. 94. $1.00.

Life of James H. Coffin, LL.D., for twenty-seven years Professor of Mathematics and Astronomy in Lafayette College; Member of the National Academy of Sciences, and other learned bodies; Discoverer of the laws which govern the Winds of the Globe. 1881, pp. 375. $1.50.

www.ingramcontent.com/pod-product-compliance
Lightning Source LLC
Chambersburg PA
CBHW022150020726
47496CB00008B/2648